DEMCO

Polly

*Also by Mary Christner Borntrager
in Large Print:*

Andy
Annie
Daniel
Ellie
Rachel
Rebecca
Reuben

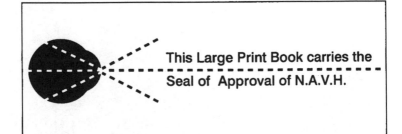

POLLY

Mary Christner Borntrager

Thorndike Press • Waterville, Maine

Published in 2002 by arrangement with Herald Press,
a division of Mennonite Publishing House, Inc.

Thorndike Press Large Print Christian Fiction Series.

The tree indicium is a trademark of Thorndike Press.

The text of this Large Print edition is unabridged.
Other aspects of the book may vary from the original edition.

Set in 16 pt. Plantin by Rick Gundberg.

Printed in the United States on permanent paper.

Library of Congress Cataloging-in-Publication Data

Borntrager, Mary Christner, 1921–
  Polly / Mary Christner Borntrager.
    p. cm. — (Ellie's people ; v 7)
  ISBN 0-7862-4030-X (lg. print : hc : alk. paper)
    1. Fathers and daughters — Fiction. 2. Amish — Fiction.
  3. Texas — Fiction. 4. Large type books. I. Title.
  PS3552.O7544 P64 2002
  813'.54—dc21   2002016033

To my other Cathy
whom I've "adopted"
as my own

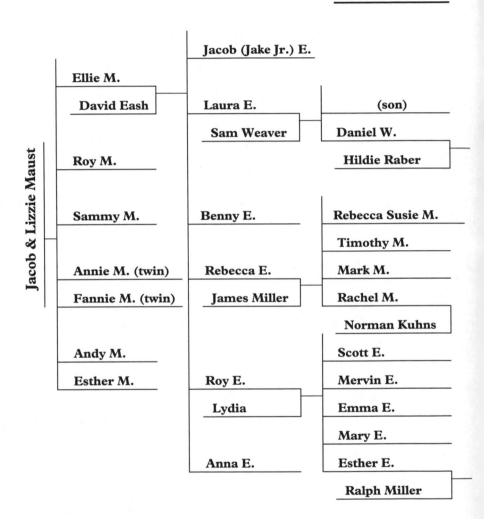

Jacob & Lizzie Maust

Ellie M.
David Eash

Roy M.

Sammy M.

Annie M. (twin)
Fannie M. (twin)

Andy M.
Esther M.

Jacob (Jake Jr.) E.

Laura E.
Sam Weaver

Benny E.

Rebecca E.
James Miller

Roy E.
Lydia

Anna E.

(son)
Daniel W.
Hildie Raber

Rebecca Susie M.
Timothy M.
Mark M.
Rachel M.
Norman Kuhns
Scott E.
Mervin E.
Emma E.
Mary E.
Esther E.
Ralph Miller

Christina Maria W.

Eli W.   Reuben W.   Henry T.

         Salome W.   Joe T.

Adam W.   Levi W.

Lucy   Jonas W.   Sarah T.

         Mandy W.   Mahlon Mast

         Samuel Troyer Edna T.

         Lizzie May W. Lisabet T.

Hannah W.

Lloyd Schrock   Susan S.   Paul T.

         Roman Troyer Joseph T.

Roseann (Rosie) W. Frieda S.   Samuel T.

         Ruth S.   Leon T.

Polly M.   Barbara S.   Annie
                 (Pearlie Mae Streeter)
Ben M.   Esther S.

Sara M.   Mandy S.   Lucy T.

Levi M.   Lloyd S.   Bertha T.

Effie M.   Jonas S.   Esther T.

William M.

Contents

1

Startling News

Polly was sad yet excited. This very morning at the breakfast table, her father had told the family that they were moving to Texas. That meant they would leave the big white farmhouse where Polly was born and had lived all her eleven years.

A great-granddaughter of Ellie, Polly felt secure in her circle of *Freindschaft* (relatives), Ellie's people. She lived near many cousins and loved visiting back and forth with them. Now her dad said they were moving out. Why?

Esther Miller looked startled at her husband's announcement. She knew that Ralph felt the young folks from their church were becoming wild and worldly, and that he wanted to protect his children from that.

A month ago, Ralph had taken the train to a place called Lone Prairie, Texas. However, since there was no Amish community in that area, she had not given it much thought. Not until now.

"But, Ralph, you said there is no Amish settlement there!" Esther exclaimed.

"Then we'll start one."

"But I —"

"We won't discuss it further. Not in front of the children." His voice was firm.

Polly was the oldest of the Miller children. Her brother Ben was two years younger. The family was filled out with Sara of age six, Levi of four and a half, Effie of two years, and baby William.

Esther had her hands full to feed, sew, and clean for a husband and six little ones. Like all their cousins, they were taught at an early age to share in the work. In the house, the barn, the garden, and the fields, the family members were used to working together as they were able.

"Mother," Polly asked after her father left the kitchen, "what will happen to our house? Who will live here? What about Pet and Patty [horses], and Spot and the other cows? Oh, yes, and Buster [their dog]?"

"*Ach* (oh), my!" replied Esther, "I don't know. Things are happening so *schnell* (quickly). *Kumm, wesch's Gscharr* (come, wash the dishes). Sara, you dry the dishes for Polly."

"Why do you always get to wash?" complained Sara.

"Because I'm the oldest and the smartest," Polly smirked.

"You are not!" Sara protested.

"I am so the oldest," insisted Polly.

"*Ya* (yes), but not the smartest."

Just then Mother broke up the debate. "*Ach, Kinner* (oh, children), don't argue. I have enough on my mind without trying to settle your fussing. Get on with your work."

Once their mom was out of earshot, Polly continued, "Alright, Sara, if you're so smart, tell me why we're moving to a state called Texas?"

"I don't know, but you don't either. Mom said there are no Amish people living at Lo . . . Low . . . something."

"You mean Lone Prairie," Polly reminded her. "That's where Dad went when he was scouting for a good place."

"*Ya,* Lone Prairie," Sara went on. "Do you think we can take Buster? I would hate him *hinnerlosse* (to leave him behind)."

"So would I." At least the two sisters agreed on that, and they were sure of support from Ben and Levi.

Meanwhile, their mother was straightening up the parlor and pondering this coming upheaval. Esther was glad her husband was concerned about the spiritual welfare of their children. Yet she wondered if they couldn't bring them up according to the Bible and their church right here in Ohio.

Surely there were temptations wherever one lived. She believed that the Lord's eyes are watching over his people anywhere. However, Esther was a faithful wife, submissive to her husband. She would follow his lead.

Late that evening Ralph told Esther, "I won't sell our farm here. We'll rent it and move to Texas for a few years. I'll have work on a large chicken and dairy farm.

"There will be work enough for both of us and the children old enough to help. We'll all be paid wages. Our house will be furnished as part payment, and we can have all the eggs and milk we need. Mr. Olson said he would even throw in a side of beef. Esther, it sounds like a good deal to me."

"But Ralph, we don't know this Mr. Olson. How can we be sure he'll keep his word?"

"*Ach, druwwle dich net* (oh, don't trouble yourself about it), Esther. He's drawing up a paper for us all to sign in the presence of witnesses."

"*Die Kinner* (the children) won't have any Amish playmates. And what about school? They'll have to go to public school. *Ach,* Ralph, are you sure this is a good move?"

"Of course I am," he assured his wife, "or we wouldn't be going. We can manage our children better once we have our own church and set rules as we see best. Sylvanus Yoders and Noah Yutzys are also talking of going. So you see, we wouldn't be without friends from home very long."

Esther drew a deep sigh. "Well, I guess you know best." At least she hoped he did.

The Miller children had all been sent to bed earlier. But Polly, sensing her parents would discuss this matter, was eavesdropping. She stretched out on the bedroom floor with one ear plastered to the register above the living room and listened.

As the conversation progressed, she became more excited, especially when she heard that they would come back someday. Back to this house which had always been home. She wondered if she could keep some of the money paid for her share of working for Mr. Olson.

"Come on to bed," Sara urged. "What are you doing on the floor, anyway?"

"Shh, be quiet!" Polly whispered. "Stay where you are, and I'll tell you pretty soon."

The two girls shared a bed. Now with only one body in the bed, Sara's feet were getting cold, and she wished her sister would hurry. But she waited silently.

Finally Polly tiptoed softly to bed. "If you don't tell me what you were doing," threatened Sara, "I'll tell Mom on you!"

"I'm going to tell you, so just be quiet. I was listening to Mom and Dad talk about moving. I don't think Mom wants to go. Dad says we won't sell this house. Someday we'll come back and live in it again.

"Oh, Sara, that makes me glad that we'll come back. We're going to work for a man called Mr. Olson. He will even pay us children for working for him."

"Really?" squealed Sara.

"Shh!" Polly shushed Sara, but it was too late.

Ralph heard his daughter's eager voice and called out, "You girls be quiet! If I have to come *dattnuff* (up there), it won't be for nothing!"

They both knew what that meant. Snuggling deep under the covers, they continued whispering until Sara's feet were toasty warm and Polly's eyes began to droop.

As the night deepened, they drifted into slumber and dreamed as little girls dream. They slept on pink clouds floating across a prairie of waving flowers and soft gentle breezes.

If they only knew what lay ahead!

2

The Less Said

News quickly spread through the Amish community that Ralph Millers were moving to Texas. This was a major item of conversation. The next Sunday after church service, women flocked around Esther with many questions and words of comfort.

"*Ach* my, so far you go now!" remarked Lucy Marner.

"Do you want to leave?" asked Elva Stuckey.

Esther replied, "I want to do what Ralph thinks is best."

The men, too, asked many things of Ralph.

"How does the land look in Texas? Is it true that it's rich in oil? How large a dairy will you be working at? Why does this Olson fellow have a poultry business, too? Doesn't one major operation supply his needs?"

"Well," laughed Omar Troyer, "you know they do things big in Texas."

"*Ya,*" Joe Stutzman agreed. "We'll let

Ralph lead the way. If he doesn't get his nose clipped, we might follow."

"What you gonna do with your farm? *Blaane du verkaffe* (are you planning to sell)?" Mose Plank asked.

"No, I'm going to rent it with all the implements included. The livestock and some household goods will go on public auction. I need to find someone dependable to handle the farm."

Young Amos Beachy heard Ralph say he would rent his farm out. He lost no time in putting in his bid for it. Recently married, Amos was looking for just such a chance.

"Come over to my place tomorrow evening and we'll talk," Ralph suggested.

Amos was elated. He could hardly wait to tell his young bride.

Polly's little friends were also throwing many questions her way.

"*Is es waahr* (is it true)? Are you moving? How far is it to Texas? Do you want to go? Why are you leaving? Will you live there forever and ever? How big is the house you will get? These people you're working for, do they have children?"

Polly couldn't answer all the questions fast enough. She didn't even know all the answers. But she was starting to put a few things together.

"I think we're moving because my dad wants a better church, and to make money so he can pay off our farm here in Ohio." This was information she had gleaned while eavesdropping.

"Why would he want a better *Gmee* (church)?" asked Lydia Mast. "What's wrong with this one?"

"I don't know, but I heard him say some people are getting too worldly."

"*Was meint sell* (what does that mean)?" Rachel Kaufman wondered.

"I guess it means fancy," Polly told her, then quickly added, "but I'm not so sure."

Of all her little Amish friends, Polly was the one with the most vivid imagination. Often while visiting on in-between Sundays (the Sunday of no church service), Polly would lead whoever she could persuade to help in playacting.

A born leader, she would take matters in hand, and the girls loved it. They would generally play house or church. Wedding was their favorite and, of course, Polly was always the bride.

Once Louella Fry, who went to a public school, told them the story of Cinderella. Polly directed that play so often until she almost wore it out.

The setting might be in her upstairs bedroom or at another friend's home where they performed in an empty corncrib. Once they gave their rendition of Cinderella behind the chicken house.

Now, however, all this was pushed aside. Polly had more important matters to discuss with her little friends and cousins.

"Do you really want to go?" Lydia asked once more.

"*Ya und nah* (yes and no)," Polly answered.

"Well, what kind of an answer is that?" Rachel laughed.

"It will be hard to leave all of you, but I want to see what Texas looks like. Besides, I've never had a train ride, and we'll be going by train. Dad said so," Polly declared importantly, with just a trace of feeling proud.

This all took place on an afternoon after the Sunday service in a farmhouse, and after the fellowship meal. The girls sought privacy in an upstairs bedroom. The Miller's relocation was certainly big news for them to think about and talk over.

"Well, I don't know if I'd want to move away from here, even if I'd get a train ride," remarked Ada Glick. She had been quietly listening to the conversation. "Here we're with our friends and relatives. We know we are safe and secure."

Some of the girls began to whisper, and

Polly suspected it was about her. She was saved from their rudeness by a summons from her mother through an older girl.

"Polly," she called, "your mother says to tell you to come. They're ready to go home."

Polly tilted her head with her nose in the air and walked out of the room as though to say, *I don't care. Your whispering doesn't bother me.* But it did.

Perhaps that is why she confided in her brother Ben on their way home. Polly and Ben had to share a ride in the back buggy box. This was a space behind the front seat, where her parents sat.

Mother held baby William on her lap. Effie and Sara shared a seat on a small bench with their backs against the dashboard. Levi sat between his parents.

It was rather crowded, but they made do, and their style of travel showed that they really were a close family. Ralph had decided to wait to buy a surrey (two-seated buggy) until they reached Texas. He would need to have one shipped from Ohio, and he thought it would be wiser to let the carriage makers prepare the surrey for shipping.

"Ben," wondered Polly, "did the boys ask you a lot of questions today about us moving?"

"Only about a zillion."

"Well, the girls asked me two zillion then!"

They were driving down the gravel road and glad their voices were concealed by the noise. Well they knew that if their parents heard them, they would be rebuked for exaggerating. How often they heard the words, "*Schteh bei die Waahret* (stand by the truth)."

"What did they say to you?" Polly asked.

"Oh, just if I want to move, why are we leaving, when are we going, how far is it, do I know there are big rattlesnakes in Texas, and —"

That's as far as her brother got when Polly let out a shriek. "*Ach,* Ben, are there really?"

Ralph pulled to the side of the road and stopped his horse. "Whoa, Cap. What's going on back there?" he demanded to know.

"Ben said some of the boys asked if he knows there are big rattlesnakes in Texas," Polly explained, "and that made me *greische* (yell)."

"Were you children telling everything about moving?" Ralph asked rather sternly.

"They asked us," Ben replied.

"Well, from now on just tell them your dad will take care of it. They don't need to know all the details. The less said the better, I always figure." Their dad flicked the reins over Cap's back, and they went on their way again.

"Are there?" Polly whispered to Ben.

"Are there what?"

"Snakes?"

"I don't know. Ask Dad."

Polly wondered and wondered about this. She did not ask her father, for he had told them, "The less said the better!"

3

Under Your Bonnet

Monday night came, and with it came Amos Beachy. He lost no time getting to the Millers' place, for he wanted to strike a deal to rent their farm.

Polly likewise lost no time placing herself on top of the register as the children were sent to bed. This was the only way she had of finding out more about Father's plans.

"Let me listen, too," Sara begged.

"No!" whispered Polly. "You *gwieke* (squeak) when you walk, and they may hear you."

"I do not *gwieke*," her sister protested.

"The floor does, though, because you don't go on your tiptoes."

"I'll be careful," Sara promised.

"No." Polly was shaking her head.

"If you don't let me, I'll tell on you."

Polly knew Sara would, too. Rather than go to bed and miss the news, she gave in to her sister. "Walk very quietly then," she told her.

Polly held her breath as Sara slowly inched toward her. She moved over to make room, then placed her finger to her lips to remind Sara to be quiet. This was exciting!

"Now, Amos," their dad began, "I guess we'd better get down to brass tacks."

"What're brass tacks?" Sara asked Polly. "We use tacks to hang fly paper and *annere soiche* (other such things)."

"*Sei schtill* (be quiet)!" Polly ordered. "If you keep talking, we can't hear what they say."

Sara gave her sister a disgusted look. She decided if she wanted to stay and spy, she needed to do as Polly said.

"Do you mean you would let me use your farm implements while you're gone if I rent your farm?" Amos asked.

"Those are my plans," Ralph answered. "Of course, I expect you to take good care of them. There will be normal wear, but keep the machinery well oiled and looking good. If anything gets broken, I expect it to be repaired or replaced. Things should be kept in working order as good as they are when I leave them."

"I understand. Then you *do* plan to come back again."

"Yes."

"Do you have any idea how soon?"

"It all depends how things go in Texas. If it works out as I think it will, I'd judge we may be back in five years or so."

At that remark Sara made a happy little noise.

"What was that?" Ralph asked his wife, who had been sitting quietly listening as she mended stockings.

Esther had heard it also. She was sure it came from her daughters' upstairs room. "I'll go and see," she offered.

This was a clue for Polly and Sara to get into bed. By the time Mother opened their bedroom door, they were both under the covers, faking sleep. The wick in the kerosene lamp was turned down low. Everything seemed to be in order.

"Are the children all in bed?" Ralph asked as Esther reentered the living room.

"*Ya,*" she reported, "*alles is ruhich* (all is quiet)."

Amos and Ralph continued negotiating their deal, but this time Polly wasn't in on it.

"*Na gucke was du geduh hoscht* (now look what you've done)," she accused her sister. "I knew I shouldn't have let you listen. You spoil everything." She poked Sara with her foot.

"Stop that!" whined Sara. "I didn't mean to make any noise. It just made me glad to

26

hear Dad say we're coming back here again. But five years is a long time. How old will I be in five years?"

"You are six now," Polly replied. "In five more years you will be eleven."

"That's as old as you are now."

"Shh! Be quiet or Mom will come up here again. Worse yet, Dad might."

That thought frightened Sara enough to bring results. She settled down close to her sister and fell asleep.

Sleep didn't come as readily for Polly. Her imagination ran wild. Far into the night, she tried to picture what their new home would be like. The school — would her teacher be as kind as Miss Byler?

What about their faithful dog, Buster? Surely Dad would take him along. She would ask her brother. Ben knew everything. Well, maybe not everything, but a lot. He spent much more time with Father than she did. Perhaps Dad talked to Ben about moving. At last, as the clock struck two, Polly slept.

"Today you will help Mom and Polly clean the henhouse," Ralph informed his son.

That was one job Ben hated, but he knew there was no getting out of it.

"I don't like it either," Polly told him when he complained to her. "But there's no use grumbling. We have to do it."

"I know, but can't I wish we wouldn't have to?"

"We'd better get used to it if we're going to work on a chicken farm in Texas," Polly stated.

"How do you know that?" Her brother was astonished.

"I heard Dad tell Mom so."

"When?" asked Ben.

"After they sent us to bed, I listened through the floor register in my room."

"*Du hoscht net* (you didn't)!" Ben exclaimed. "Now you'll get a *Bletsching* (spanking)."

"Not if they don't find out. You won't tell, will you?" Polly asked, terrified at the thought.

"Tell me what you heard, and I promise to be quiet."

Polly was relieved. "I listened at the register twice — once when Dad and Mom were talking, and then when Amos Beachy came to see Dad about renting the farm."

"Polly, how did you dare? What if they found out? Does Sara know?" Ben asked.

"*Ya,* she listened too one time."

Now her brother *was* surprised.

"Didn't Dad tell you anything about where we are going and what we will do there?" Polly asked.

"Well, yes, he did and he didn't."

"*Ach,* Ben, *du machst ken Verschtand* (oh, you don't make any sense). How could he tell you and yet not tell you?"

"Well, I was in town with him when Ora Schrock came to our buggy just as we were leaving. He stopped Dad and asked him a lot of questions. So I found out we will be working for a man named Mr. Olson. He has a big chicken and dairy farm.

"Olson will pay all of us to work for him. I hope I can work on the dairy. I like cows better than dumb old clucking hens. But now don't you say a word of this to anyone, mind you! Dad told me to keep it under my hat. So you keep it under your bonnet."

"*Kummt, Kinner* (come, children)," Esther called from across the yard. Obediently they followed her to the henhouse.

Polly wanted to find out more from her brother, but she would wait. What she already knew she must keep under her bonnet.

4

The Truth Comes Out

Everyone wanted to invite the Ralph Miller family for an in-between Sunday dinner (the alternate Sunday with no services) before they left the community. It was not unusual for them to receive several invitations for the same Sunday.

Sometimes Esther was almost too tired to go. These were busy days for her, with so many decisions to make. What should she take to their new home? What was best to sell at the auction?

Those old enough to help were all busy sorting, packing, labeling, and storing. Esther was truly glad for a large attic. Here she would keep many things which she could not take when they moved.

At times Polly felt as if her legs could not carry her up those steps one more time. She never liked that dark old place. Sometimes wasps had built nests in the rafters. Once she got stung right on top of her head.

"Mom, do I have to go up to the attic again?" she groaned over and over. "Why can't Sara go this time?"

"Sara is not as strong as you are. *Mach schnell nau* (go quickly now). We can't waste *Zeit* (time)."

"But there are *Weschbe* (wasps) up there," Polly griped.

"*Ach,* Dad sprayed them, and I don't think you'll see any more."

Cautiously Polly took a box of good dishes and trudged up the steps as before. Mother said they would only take the everyday dishes to save on space and, of course, expenses.

"But what if we get company in our new home?" Polly asked. "We won't have good dishes to set a nice table."

"I know," her mother replied. "I thought of that, too, but Dad says food tastes just as good eaten from our regular plates."

"Why doesn't he tell us about moving and our new home, Mom?" Polly complained.

"He says people talk too much and soon things get all *verhuddelt* (mixed up)."

"Well, I wouldn't tell. I and Ben and Sara wonder if we can take Buster. Will we get paid real money for working? Do I work with Mr. Olson's chickens or the cows? I don't know

31

much about cows, but Ben says he wants to work in the dairy."

"Polly!" exclaimed Mother. "Where did you find out there will be a dairy-and-chicken farm to work on? Who told you about getting paid?"

Only then did Polly realize the mistake she had made. She hung her head and felt hot all over.

"Answer me, Polly," Esther demanded.

Mother did not speak sternly as Father would have done, but she did speak with shock and surprise.

"We listened."

"Listened where?"

"At the upstairs register. Mom, I know we shouldn't have, but we didn't know what would happen to us." A tear or two trickled down Polly's cheek. "Are you going to tell Dad?" She was trembling.

"No," her mom decided. "What's done is done. Your dad has enough on his mind. Only don't sneak around again, listening to things not for your ears. You don't need to be afraid of what will happen. Dad and I will take care of you. Did Ben eavesdrop too?"

"No, Mom, just Sara and I."

"Did you tell him about it?"

"Yes, I did, but he said he won't tell."

"Well, Polly," Esther stated, "you can't do

wrong and get by with it. Sooner or later your sin will be found out. This time you told on yourself. You did wrong, and I don't want it to happen again. I can understand that you wanted to know what was going on. But, Polly, just trust us. We'll tell you what we feel is necessary."

Polly was ever so grateful for her mother's kind understanding in not reporting her to her dad.

"Now get the irons out and start the ironing." There were two baskets full needing to be done before Sunday.

The sadirons Polly worked with were heavy. She had to heat them on the cookstove. She used a detachable handle to pick up a flat iron and iron with it while the others were being heated for their turn on the ironing board. Polly's arms often ached from doing this task.

The clothes had been dampened the night before and rolled into tight little bundles. In spite of the hard work, Polly liked to iron, especially flat pieces such as hankies or tea towels. While she worked, she could think of many things. She was almost glad mother knew how she had eavesdropped.

"Where are we going for Sunday dinner this time?" Polly asked her mother.

"To Elam Frey's, I guess. Elizabeth asked

me first after church."

"Who else asked."

"*Ach,* my, Lucy Marner, Lavina Mast, and Mattie Stutzman."

"Well, I'm glad we are going to Elam's," Polly responded. "I like to play with Louella. She's so much fun."

"But she has a lot of *englisch* (non-Amish) ideas since she goes to public school, Polly. I hope you don't get such notions in your head."

As she worked, Polly began planning for next Sunday and the play they could do. It would be Cinderella. Once more before moving away, Polly wanted to be Cinderella. She would try to get her brother to play the part of the prince — if he would cooperate.

"Look once what you're doing, Polly!" Esther warned. "You've almost burned a hole in Dad's good white shirt. Why do you let the iron sit so long in one spot? *Ach,* my! It's scorched brown, and it's the only Sunday shirt he has. *Was is dir letz* (what's wrong with you)?

"Now with all my other work, I'll have to make a new shirt for dad before next church services. Well, I'll just have to get a *Maut* (hired girl). That's all there is to it. Pay attention to what you're doing."

"*Ya,* Mom," Polly answered. She was truly

sorry, especially after her mother had been so kind, forgiving her for listening to private conversations.

That evening at the supper table, Esther raised the question with her husband. "I'm getting so worn out, I'd like to have a *Maut*."

"Do you really think you need one?"

"Oh, yes, I sure do, what with getting ready to move and all."

"Then see if you can find one. Don't get a fancy one, but one I can afford."

Polly wondered who this would be. Sara asked where they would put her.

"You'll have to share your room," Mother told her girls.

When Ben had a chance, he warned Polly not to try to eavesdrop if they had a *Maut*. "She might tell Mom."

"Oh, I won't," Polly promised. "Anyway, Mom already knows."

"But how? How did she find out?" Ben was surprised.

"Oh, I told on myself."

"But *why?*"

5

Chicken Coop Playhouse

Polly had Ben right where she wanted him. He couldn't understand why she told on herself. Now if Ben wanted to know, he would have to be in her play on Sunday.

"Come on, Polly, tell me," he begged.

"Huh-uh, wait till Sunday."

"But why Sunday? Tell me now —"

"No, I'll tell you when I'm ready."

"I don't see why you won't tell me." Ben was exasperated.

"I have my reasons. You'll see."

Sunday finally came, and by eleven o'clock the Miller family was on their way to Elam Frey's for dinner. Polly and Ben were in their usual place in the back buggy box.

The weather was still warm enough so the back curtain was rolled up. The children loved to dangle their bare feet out the back. It was so much more comfortable. Besides, according to Dad, it saved shoe leather and *Geld* (money).

"Tell me now what you meant when you said you told Mom," Ben insisted as they rode along.

"No, Ben, Dad might hear us. I'll tell you after dinner."

"You can whisper it. I'll listen real good," her brother coaxed.

"No, I won't. Be quiet and let me be. Look at that *Summer Fliegli* (butterfly). Isn't it pretty? It's yellow and black. Why, Ben, I've never seen such a big one before. Look, it sat on that goldenrod flower! Oh, I wish we could catch it. Miss Byler [her teacher] says they drink nectar from flowers. I wonder what nectar tastes like."

Polly chattered on, but Ben paid no attention. He thought, *How stubborn Polly is sometimes.*

It was early September, and the goldenrod heads were beginning to show their color. Wild grapes graced the fences along the roadside. Soon school bells would be ringing, calling children back to class.

Polly wondered if she could go to Moss Hill one more time. Maybe Father wouldn't mind if she asked him.

Her thoughts turned to other things as they neared the Frey homestead. She saw that other company had arrived just ahead of them. *Oh, goody! Rachel Kaufman and her parents are here. Rachel is always fun.*

The Kaufmans only had one son, and he was just three years old, too young to play with Ben. Eddie and Paul Frey were older, so Ben felt rather alone.

"Come right in, Ralph," Elam called out as they stepped from their buggy. "My boys will take care of your horse. They have to see to Levi's rig anyway."

Sadie Kaufman and Esther Miller had already greeted each other and made their way inside.

"Just come on in." Mrs. Frey wiped her hands on a towel and shook the dust off her apron. "Dinner is almost ready. As soon as Omar Troyers get here, we can eat."

When Ben heard her say this, it pleased him that Omars were coming. They had a boy his own age.

"Take the babies to the living room, girls, and play with them until we get dinner on," suggested Lena Frey.

Polly liked to watch her little brother if he wasn't *gridlich* (fussy). Louella picked up her baby sister and told Polly to follow her.

No sooner were they seated on the floor with their charges when Polly heard Elam say, "So, Ralph, you're selling out. What's wrong? Too hard to get your farm paid off?"

This was not what Ralph wanted to hear.

Did people think he wasn't a good manager? It seemed to him Elam was smirking.

"No, I'm not selling out. We're keeping the farm. I've rented it out for a while."

"Are you sure it's the thing to do?" Levi Kaufman asked.

"We'll see." Ralph was glad to hear Elam's wife announce Omar Troyer's arrival.

"As soon as everyone comes inside, we'll eat," she announced.

What a meal they had. After everyone had eaten plenty, the women took their babies and the girls did the dishes. Louella had a grown sister who supervised the kitchen work.

Now came the moment Polly had been waiting for.

"What do you girls want to do?" Louella asked her guests.

"Let's do the play Cinderella. I'll be Cinderella, and I'm going to ask my brother Ben to be the Prince," Polly told them.

"*Ach,* he won't do it," objected Rachel Kaufman.

"Well, I'll just bet he will. There's something he wants me to tell him, and I won't unless he does as I say." The other girls looked astonished.

"You go upstairs and get things ready, and I'll get Ben."

Polly found Ben and Ervin Troyer by the goldfish pond and tried to hook a fish for herself, in a sense. "Ben, if you come with me now, I'll tell you how I tattled on myself."

Ervin looked puzzled as he followed Ben and Polly. He never heard of anyone tattling on themselves.

Before Polly reached the house, the other girls met her outside. "We can't do our play upstairs," Louella told her.

"Why not?"

"The *Yunge* (young folks) are up there playing the victrola, and they don't want to be disturbed."

"What's a victrola?" Polly wondered.

"It makes music. You put a record on, and music comes out."

"Are they allowed to have it? My dad says music is worldly."

"They aren't members of the *Gmee* (church) yet. But once they're baptized, they can't have it."

"Well, then where can we go to do our play?"

"We could use our large chicken coop. It's empty. It's really a brooder house for baby chicks."

"Let's go then," Polly agreed. "But I need a sheet or shawl for dress-up."

"What are you doing?" Ben asked.

"We are giving a play called 'Cinderella.' You're going to be the prince."

"Oh no, I'm not," protested Ben.

"Then I won't tell you what I told Mom," Polly threatened.

"I don't care. It's not important enough to make me be in your silly old play."

"See," giggled Rachel, "I told you he wouldn't."

"Let him go. Who needs him anyway? We'll just play several parts. I'll use my apron for a veil when I'm Cinderella. We'll just have a pretend prince."

Polly knew this might be her last performance with her little friends, so she made it her best one ever. To the girls it was grand, even with the chicken coop as a stage.

6

The Maut

Polly was all ears on the ride home. She kept catching snatches of conversation about moving, and she listened intently.

"*Ya,*" commented her dad, "some of the men are changing their tune. I believe Omar Troyer is thinking of checking into a Texas deal, too. Did you hear what Levi Kaufman asked me to do? He wants me to let him know how things go for us. I suspect that means that if all goes well, the Kaufmans might come too."

Esther nodded. "*Ach,* maybe." Then she asked the questions Polly had been waiting to hear. "Ralph, how soon are we moving? *Wann kann ich en Maut hawwe* (when can I have a hired girl) to help us get ready?"

Polly, standing instead of sitting, heard every word.

"I figure we'll leave within a month. You can get a *Maut* next week if you think you need her this far ahead. It takes *Geld* (money), and I heard they're asking higher wages now.

"Today Elam was boasting that one of their daughters brought home ten dollars for only one week's work. That would cost forty dollars if we had a *Maut* for a month," Ralph quickly calculated. "Try to get someone for less. We have to watch our pennies. *Geld waxe net uff Beem* (money doesn't grow on trees)."

Esther felt almost guilty. If only she could get things done without outside help. Her husband worked so hard to support his family.

"I'll try, Ralph. I'll try to get someone who won't overcharge us. Maybe if I work a little harder, we won't need her four weeks."

"I hope not," Ralph returned.

Monday morning Esther called her daughter from her work in the kitchen. "Polly, let Sara finish the dishes, and you take this note to Jake's. Wait for an answer."

Jake Neffs were neighbors to the Millers. They would often borrow and lend and visit back and forth. Several of their daughters worked for other Amish families. Esther just hoped one was available. She preferred the oldest one, known to be an excellent worker.

Polly gladly ran the errand — anything to get out of doing dishes. Soon she was back with the answer. Handing her mother the return note, Polly waited to hear the results.

"Well," commented Esther, "I really wanted Dora, but I'll just be glad to get any help."

That is how it came about that Katie Neff arrived at the Miller's right after breakfast on Tuesday morning.

"I would have come earlier, but Dad said they needed me to help chore. He won't charge you full price since I won't be choring here. Dad wondered if six dollars a week sounds fair. I won't be eating here either, except at noon."

The reduction in price pleased Ralph. He was not a miser, but he believed in thrift and good management.

"*Ya, des is gut* (this is good)." Ralph looked pleased.

Esther was happy that her husband approved.

"Where do you want me to begin?" Katie asked.

Esther could see that she was willing to start right away.

"It's nice out today, so you and Polly wash windows. Then the strawberry patch needs to be weeded one more time and covered with straw for the winter. After that, you can rake leaves. We must clean up for the sale day."

Polly was delighted to work alongside the *Maut*. She cleaned the lower windowpanes while Katie used a ladder to reach the higher ones.

"Help me move the ladder, Polly."

Polly gladly obliged. She chattered every chance she had.

"You know, we're going to have lots of work in Texas," Polly reported. "We will all be paid for working. Even I and Ben and maybe Sara, if she can help." Polly looked important.

"Oh, yeah? Who told you that?"

"No one," she answered mysteriously.

"Then how do you know?"

"I heard my dad tell Mom about that when I listened from the floor register in my bedroom."

"*Ach,* Polly, you shouldn't spy on others."

"I didn't spy; I only listened."

"Same thing," Katie insisted. "We'd better keep working or we won't get to the strawberry patch or leaf-raking. You *babble* (chatter) too much."

"Well, I can work while I talk," Polly defended herself. "Sometimes I even work faster when I'm talking."

By noon the girls had the windows sparkling and three-fourths of the berry patch cleaned. Ben wasn't at all pleased when his mother asked if he could be spared to help haul straw to cover the plants.

"If it doesn't take too long. I need him most of the afternoon," his dad stated. "You may use Pet (a horse) and the cart to haul the straw to the garden."

Several times Katie tried to strike up a conversation with Ben, but he was shy — sure not like his sister Polly. Ben worked as fast as he could, and soon the job of hauling straw was done.

Katie liked to sing while she worked. Polly loved it. She heard songs she had never heard before. Her mom usually sang the German songs. They were much slower paced and had many words which Polly couldn't understand.

Katie sang about an "Old Rugged Cross," "I Shall Not Be Moved," and many others. How Polly wished she could remember them. Her father, however, was not so pleased.

"Doesn't she do anything without singing?" he asked his wife.

"She's an excellent worker. I believe she gets as much done in a day as her sister Dora can. As long as she does her job, I don't mind her singing. Rather sing than *brutze* (pout)," Esther replied.

The four weeks passed quickly, and the Millers were busy indeed. Esther would not be guilty of leaving behind anything less than a spotless house.

The day of the sale came and went. With it went a few cherished pieces of furniture which Esther had to let go. She shed some tears as reality hit her. Friends and relatives gathered around to comfort her.

Polly, too, had mixed feelings. It was an exciting time yet also uncertain. She had asked their hired girl if there really were big snakes in Texas. The kind *Maut* tried to put her mind at ease. She told her that the boys who told Ben about the snakes were only trying to scare them.

Then the hired girl began to sing. That always made Polly feel better. Perhaps now if Polly sang when her mother was sad, it would help. Loudly and off key, Polly sang, "I shall not be, I shall not be blue."

"No, no," Katie laughed. "It's 'I shall not be moved.' I'll sing with you." What a good *Maut!*

47

7

The Last Good-Byes

It all seemed so strange to Polly. The day after the sale, things looked so different. She did not need to gather eggs from the henhouse.

The cow stables, too, were empty. Her brindle cow and all the cows were gone. Only a few young pullets and Buster the dog were left. The pullets had not started laying eggs yet.

"Ben," observed Polly, "it doesn't seem as if we live here anymore."

"Well, we won't be here for long," her brother replied.

"Dad said we're moving out on Monday."

"Do you want to go?" Polly asked. She wanted assurance that things would turn out alright. If Ben wanted to leave, then she would be more confident about the move.

In Polly's eyes, Ben was smart even if he could be stubborn. But asking him didn't help, for he only responded, "In some ways, yes, I want to."

"But what about the other ways?" Polly prodded him.

"I'll miss our cousins and the school. But then, I guess we'll go to school in Texas and make friends."

"What if they do have big snakes out there?" Polly asked.

"I'll believe it once I see it," Ben answered.

"Did Dad say yet if we're taking Buster?"

"Well, he didn't sell him at our sale, so I hope we can take him."

"I do, too. He's been our dog all his life. He wouldn't know anyone else."

Polly could wait no longer. At supper that evening, she approached her father. "Dad, are we taking Buster with us when we move out?"

"*Sicher net* (certainly not)! The train fare will cost enough without dragging a dog along." Ralph eyed his daughter reproachfully, as if to say, *You should know better.*

"But, Dad, it isn't just a dog — it's Buster. He's part of our family."

"Watch your mouth. The *Schrift* (Scripture) says, 'Children, obey your parents.' Also, 'honor your father and mother.' I'll have no back talk."

Esther saw the downcast, tearful eyes of her

49

daughter and soothed her with a few words. "Buster will be here where he always has been. This is his home. Amos Beachys are kind people. They will take good care of him until we come back."

Polly longed to ask if Buster wouldn't miss them. Her father had made it clear that she must not question their decisions. Polly swallowed hard and kept silent for now.

After they arrived in Texas, she planned to ask Mother to write to Mrs. Beachy and find out how Buster was doing. For now, there were many duties to attend to.

Polly, Ben, and the other children old enough to help, packed box after box. Neighbors and relatives came to lend a hand with the moving.

"We want to have a special singing yet before you leave," Lovina Mast told Esther.

"Oh, my, when is this?" Esther exclaimed.

"You're leaving on Monday, isn't that right?"

"*Ya, sel is so* (that's so)."

"I'm inviting you for Sunday evening supper. You have most everything packed up, so you come. After supper the *Freindschaft* (relatives) and neighbors will come to sing a while and say good-bye. They'll also bring ice cream and cake. They wouldn't let me make dessert."

"*Ach,* my," protested Esther. "You go to way too much fuss."

"It's no bother when it's for a friend. We'll enjoy the singing."

Lovina did not tell Esther what else the women were bringing. That must be a surprise.

Ralph wasn't pleased when his wife told him of this invitation to the Mast home. He was exhausted from the hard work of preparing for auction, attending to many matters during the auction, and getting their freight ready for the train.

"I'm tired and would rather stay at home," he told his wife. "You would think people could know we need our rest. Here we are, ready to move out, and they keep us going until the last minute."

"I'm tired, too," Esther responded. "But with most of our things packed away, I'm glad I don't need to cook supper. Some of the people are bringing cake and ice cream. Then we're having a singing. Oh, yes, Lovina wants us to bring along our *Liedersammlung* (thin German songbook) if we haven't packed it yet."

"Oh, sure, we'll go if there is to be a singing," Ralph declared. If there was one thing he enjoyed, it was singing. He was a good singer and often led out in church services.

At services, Ralph was often the one to sing the first word of each line alone. Then the others joined in. Ralph had an excellent voice that carried well. Now he looked forward to this last singing session before they moved.

The Miller children were also eager for Sunday to come. To them, one day now seemed like a week. On Saturday, Esther and Polly baked cookies and half-moon pies to take along on the train in order to save on food. Come Monday morning, she would make sandwiches and pack some apples from their trees.

To prepare for Sunday, the children needed to have their hair washed and get their baths in the old tin tub. The girls' hair needed braiding, the boys needed hair cuts, and the house had to be cleaned.

This was the Sunday of no services, so the forenoon was spent in Bible reading and quiet activities. The children played a few games of hide the thimble and Quakers' meeting.

After a light lunch, Mother, Father, and the younger children took naps. Ben and Polly played fetch with Buster.

"It seems like Buster knows we're moving," commented Polly.

"No, he doesn't," Ben disagreed.

"Well, see how sad he looks, and he doesn't fetch so quickly."

"He's just tired." Yet Ben also wondered if Buster had some inkling what was about to happen.

"Come, children, it's time to go to the Masts," Mother called.

It didn't take Ben and Polly long to get ready. They always liked to get together with their friends.

What a good time they had that night! The weather was brisk but still nice enough for the children to play outside until it became dark.

After the supper dishes were cleared, the table was wiped and they gathered around with their songbooks. Esther thought she had never heard such good singing.

Since they were moving, her husband was asked to lead many songs. Finally he told them to spare his throat or he wouldn't be able to eat that good cake and ice cream. How they laughed at his joke.

Yes, everyone had a jolly time. Now it was getting late. Some of the women left the room but came back with a large bundle.

"Here, Esther," they announced. "This is for you so you won't forget us."

Esther's hands trembled and her voice broke as she unfolded a beautiful friendship quilt. Each lady had embroidered a square block with a design, her name, and a Scripture verse.

"It's for you, too, Ralph," Lovina Mast reminded them. "It will keep you both warm."

Esther was almost speechless. "*Mir sage danki* (we say thanks)," Ralph spoke for them both.

They made their good-byes, and then Ralph told his children, "We must go, for tomorrow we are moving out."

8

Schlof, Bobbli, Schlof

Polly awoke to the sound of rain spattering against her window. She poked Sara and exclaimed, "Wake up! Today we're going on the train."

Sara sat bolt upright. "I don't think I'll like a train ride. They're noisy and go like a *Schtraal Blitz* (streak of lightning)."

"Would you rather walk then?" asked Polly. "That's what you would have to do if you don't go on the train."

"I didn't say I won't. I only said I don't think I'll like it. Why do we have to do things we don't like? Is that because we're Amish?"

"*Ach, kindisch* (silly, childish). All children have to do things sometimes that they would rather not do."

"How do you know?"

"I'm older than you, so I know more."

"That doesn't make you smarter."

"*Meed* (girls), it's time to get up," Mother

called. "We have much to do, so *dummlet* (hurry)."

It was still dark outside. Polly turned the wick of the kerosene lamp up higher. Its glow cast eerie shadows on the walls.

She heard her brothers tramp downstairs. Then she heard Father come upstairs. He went to the boys' room and began to take the beds apart. A neighbor was coming early with his truck to haul beds and some other furniture to the freight depot.

"How will we get our stuff once it arrives in Texas?" asked Ben. He had returned upstairs to help his dad.

"Mr. Olson will pick it up with his truck. Now start carrying those bed slats downstairs. I'll bring the headboard and foot end. Then we'll empty the straw ticks."

"I'll need help to carry the springs down. Aren't those girls up yet? Their bed will have to be taken apart, too."

"*Meed* (girls)," Ralph called, "are you up and dressed?"

"*Ya,*" Polly answered.

"Well, *mach schnell* (hurry up) and go help Mom with breakfast. We don't have all day."

"Here, Sara, I'll button your dress," Polly offered.

Sara was glad for Polly's help. It was almost impossible for her to perform such a task

56

alone. She was still young enough to have buttons down the back of her dress. However, she knew that when she was old enough to dress like her mother, she would have to use straight pins.

As soon as the beds, bedding, a chest, and several chests of drawers were brought downstairs, the family ate a hurried breakfast.

Soon neighbors and Ralph's and Esther's parents began to arrive. There were last-minute things to take care of. Amos Beachy came with a wagonload of furniture, anxious to move right in. He and his new wife had been staying with her parents, and they were eager to set up housekeeping.

The rain had subsided, but now and again a shower sprang up.

"Polly, you help Sara and Effie fold the bed covers and put them neatly in this large box. Put the pillows in first.

"I must tell the women how I want the kitchen things done and who will get my *Blummeschteck* (flower plants) and about all my canned goods and — *ach*, well, just do those covers. There is a brown paper bag in the box. Put the folded pillowcases in it."

"But, Mom," objected Polly, "this box has holes in the side. It looks like it had oranges in it, and then the store packed groceries in it for us one time."

"That doesn't matter. It's good enough to keep covers in. Now get busy."

"Where is that Effie?" Polly exclaimed.

"She was here just a minute ago," Sara told her.

"That girl! If you don't watch her every minute, she disappears."

"I expect she's out in the barn playing with the *Busslin* (kittens)," Sara remarked. "She thinks the little black-and-white spotted one is hers."

"I know," Polly agreed. "She claims she's taking Spottie with her all the way to Texas. Oh, well, we might as well go on and fold these blankets. By the time we'd round her up, we could be halfway there."

The girls laughed and set to work. Mother had told them to leave the top of the box open in case she needed to put anything inside at the last minute.

"All done," Polly declared as she put the paper bag with pillowcases on top of the pile. "Now let's go see if we can play with Buster one more time before we leave."

Several of their cousins had arrived. Mother declared that she now had plenty of help. The children could go outside for one last romp with the family dog.

"Don't stay too long. The baby is *gridlich* (fussy). Polly, I need you to take care of him.

If it starts raining again, you come right in. I don't want you getting wet or sick."

"*Ya,* Mom," Polly answered as she, Sara, and three of their cousins ran outside just as her little sister Effie toddled toward the house. Mr. Price was already there, and Ben, Ralph, and other men were loading the truck.

The dawn was gray and foreboding. It didn't do a thing for the Miller children's spirits. They talked to Buster and tried to explain they would come back again. He looked at them with sad, forlorn eyes and slowly thumped his tail on the ground where he lay.

"Polly! Polly!" Mother called.

"I have to go in now," Polly told her cousins.

"Take Baby William once," Mother requested. "He cries so much I can't get anything done. He's afraid of the other women."

The rocker was already on the truck, so Polly couldn't rock the baby and sing as she generally did. She walked the floor with him until her arms and back ached.

"Is this box ready to go?" Ralph asked as he lifted the large one with the covers in it.

"Yes, I guess so," Esther answered.

Ralph closed the lid securely and ordered, "Take it away, boys."

It was time to leave.

"Don't look back," advised Grandpa

Miller. "It only makes it harder."

"I'll take real good care of Buster," Amos Beachy promised.

Before it seemed true, the Miller family was on the train. Rain was falling fast and hard again. Though they tried to hide them, tears were also falling from the eyes of Mother, Polly, and Sara.

Effie was scared of the train noise and whistle. Mother tried to comfort her.

"Here, Polly, you take the baby. I'll have to hold Effie until she calms down."

Baby William cried and cried. Polly thought, *If I sing for him like I did at home, it might help.* Rocking him back and forth in her arms, she began, "*Schlof, Bobbli, Schlof, der Dawdy hiede die Schof* (sleep, baby, sleep, Grandpa watches the sheep)."

Why was everyone staring at her?

9

Tomorrow for Real

"Can't you quiet that baby?" Ralph asked Polly as he leaned across the aisle.

"The children are *verhuddelt* (mixed up) with all this noise," Esther replied. "Maybe it's time for the baby's bottle. Could you go and see if there is a place to warm the milk, Ralph?"

Esther rummaged through her *Windel Schatley* (diaper bag) and handed the bottle to him.

As he made his way through the train to the dining car, Ralph was keenly aware of people staring at him, too. He knew it was because of his plain clothes, wide-brimmed hat, and whiskers. Some of these travelers had never seen Amish folks before, and they were fascinated.

One passenger was not kind at all. As Ralph approached with bottle in hand, the stranger laughed and began to bleat like a goat.

Ralph quickly rose to the occasion. Turning to the scoffer, he offered him the bottle of milk.

Instantly the bleating stopped. The man's face turned red, and Ralph continued on down the aisle, chuckling to himself.

I sure got that fellow's goat, he thought.

Polly had to care for Baby William most of the day because Effie wouldn't leave Mother's side. She was such a mama's baby. But then, she was only two.

"Mom, do I have to hold the baby all the way to Texas?" Polly asked. "My arms are getting tired."

"If I can get Effie to sit with Dad, I'll take William." The minute Esther handed Effie to Ralph, she began crying.

When her father told her to pipe down and smacked her bottom, she objected loudly. Such a commotion drew more attention. Ralph then tried to interest Effie in playing with his pocket watch, but she was too upset to pay attention to it.

"Here," he said, giving the squalling child back to Esther. "You take her. She isn't used to me. Anyhow, it's the woman's job to take care of them when they're still so small."

Wearily Polly took Baby William back in her arms so her mother could comfort Effie. "You have it easy, Ben," she told her brother, sitting one seat down from her. "All you need to do is watch the fields and towns go by."

"Yeah, but I worked harder to get ready to move than you did. That's why I need more *Ruh* (rest)."

Polly didn't agree with him but knew better than to start an argument.

A lady who had been watching Polly asked if she might hold the baby. Polly didn't know what to say. This was an *Englischer* (non-Amish) woman. Would her parents approve?

She looked at Mother. Esther nodded and smiled. With great relief Polly deposited the baby into the lady's outstretched arms.

"Oh, she is such a cute little thing," cooed the stranger. "By the way, my name is Millie Watson. You have a nice family. Are you traveling far?"

"To Texas," Esther answered.

"Oh, my! That's a long way. I'll be going about half that far. Do you mind if I help with this little girl while we travel together?"

Polly wished her mother would say yes.

"Are you sure you want to? He gets pretty fussy at times. The doctor said he has colic."

"He!" exclaimed Millie. "This baby is a boy?"

"Yes, he's a boy."

"But you dress him like a girl!"

"*Ya,* that's our way."

63

Ralph was listening to this conversation intently. He didn't care to have his family become too involved with outsiders.

Polly was happy that she was getting help in holding the baby.

Effie kept asking for her kitten, Spottie. Over and over she asked to hold Spottie.

"She'll just have to get used to the fact that Spottie is not coming with us," Ralph declared.

"*Ya,* she'll get over it," Esther agreed.

"Are we almost there?" Levi wondered. They had been traveling most of the day.

"No," Ben responded. "Dad told me we'll have to change trains sometime during the night."

"But I'm getting tired of just sitting."

"Mom's getting some sandwiches and half-moon pies out for us to eat. You'll feel better then. Do you know these seat backs lean back partway? We can sleep until we have to change trains."

The children did sleep until they pulled into the depot at three in the morning. Then the confusion and crying started all over again.

Millie Watson had been a big help. She guided the family in changing trains. Before long she had discovered why the Amish dress their boy babies like little girls. With dresses, diapers are so much easier to change, and it is simpler for training them to do without diapers.

At the depot Millie had managed to find a rack with books, small toys, and knickknacks for sale. Quickly she bought two boxes of crayons and coloring books, plus a few matchbox cars. Handing the bag with her purchases to Esther, she bid them good-bye.

"Something for the children. I must leave now. I hope you have a safe journey and will like your new home."

"Thank you," Esther replied.

The children were eager to see what the bag contained.

"Wait until we get on the train," Mother decided. "We have enough to keep track of."

"Come along, everyone." Father helped the children up the steps into the train. He, too, was anxious to get the traveling over with.

"All aboard," called out the conductor. Big puffs of smoke began to billow from the train. The engineer blew the whistle two short blasts. Slowly, as though painfully, the wheels began to move, creaking and chugging as they built up speed. Soon they were racing along once more.

"Our next stop will be Whitefield," announced Ralph. "That's where we get off.

Mr. Olson will meet us there and take us to Lone Prairie and our house. But make yourselves comfortable. We still have fourteen hours of train travel."

"Can we look now?" asked Ben.

"Look at what?" his dad wondered.

"In this bag that *Englisch* woman gave us."

"Guess we won't have any *Ruh* (rest) until you do."

Eagerly the children opened the bag to see what it held for them.

"Coloring books and crayons!" Polly exclaimed.

"*Ya,* and look," Levi chortled with glee, "little cars." He held them up for the others to admire.

"And a popgun," noted Ben.

"Give those here," Ralph commanded. "These worldly things are not for us. Today a toy car and a gun, tomorrow the real thing. You may keep the crayons. The books and cars and gun will have to go. Crayons you can use in school."

Polly's spirits fell, for she had seen that the one coloring book was called *Cinderella.*

"That's the way it is," Father stated. "Today pretend, tomorrow for real."

10

The Stowaway

"How far is it yet?" Polly asked her mother in the middle of the afternoon. Again she was tired from caring for the baby.

"We should get there before dark," Esther answered. "I hope we do. We are all tired and hungry for hot food. It will be easier to unload if it's still daylight. *Ach*, I hope our furniture will come in this evening so we can set up the beds and get to sleep early."

Finally the train slowed and the conductor called out, "Whitefield Station."

"This is where we get off," Ralph told his family.

Several other people disembarked, but none more eagerly than the Millers.

"My legs are so stiff I can't walk," Polly groaned.

"Yes, you can," Mother coaxed her. "Just stand and stretch a little."

Esther was right. Polly soon stepped from

that old smoky train. The conductor helped her, and though it embarrassed her, she was grateful for a helping hand.

A man about Ralph's age approached them. He was brown from the sun and wearing a cowboy hat.

"Well, Ralph, I see you made it. For once the 6:30 was on time. This your family?" He looked at the little group huddled together by the depot.

"Yes."

"How soon do you suppose our stuff will get here? We need our beds, table, dishes, and so on."

"Oh, those came in this afternoon. My misses and boys helped me unload, and they're in the house already. But your bed mattresses didn't arrive yet. I can't understand that."

"Oh, well, we put straw ticks on our beds for mattresses. You do have straw I could use for that?" Ralph asked.

"Well, I never!" Mr. Olson exclaimed. "Of course I have straw you can have, but it's too dark to fetch it tonight. We have some folding cots you can use for one night. Come along. It's time I get you folks put up."

He pointed a direction and picked up two suitcases. "My van is just down the street here."

Glad for his help, the family followed, lugging the rest of the bags they had brought along. Effie clung tighter to her mother. "Kitty, kitty," she sobbed, looking back at the train.

"Here we are," Mr. Olson announced as they pulled into a narrow muddy lane. The house looked small and forlorn.

The children spilled out of the van as soon as the doors opened, eager to size up this new world of Texas.

"*Wo is es heisli* (where is the outhouse)?" Sara asked.

"I don't know. I don't see any," replied her mother.

"*Was will sie* (what does she want)?" Ralph asked.

Esther told her husband.

"*Es is in haus* (it's in the house)," he informed them.

Sara was dumbfounded. Never had she heard of such a thing. What Amish family would have a toilet in the house! Yet, she followed her family inside.

Her dad pointed her to the bathroom. Mother followed with Effie. She had not been told they would have such a modern convenience. Once Sara saw how it worked, she began flushing the thing just to watch the water rushing in and out.

The other children soon discovered how to turn lights off and on. Had Ralph not put a stop to their antics, the switches would soon have worn out.

Esther and Polly wondered if they were worldly, moving into a place like this. Polly didn't really care, but Esther felt rather wicked. She must discuss this matter with her husband. He had told her little about the house.

Just then a loud clanging came from the living room. It startled Mother and the children.

"Oh, the telephone," Mr. Olson exclaimed. "Probably my wife calling." He picked up the receiver and began, "Hello."

Ben and Polly had seen telephones, but they had never spoken through one.

"It looks like we're going to live fancy," Polly told Ben.

"*Ya,* this will be fun. Maybe we will like Texas," her brother responded.

"That was the missus," Mr. Olson told Ralph and Esther. He always referred to his wife as "the missus." "She was just checking to see if you got here. I guess she'll be over to see if you need help getting settled in."

Esther just sat down in her familiar rocker, which had earlier arrived with the freight.

Mr. Olson was eager to get them oriented

to the new setting and put them to work. "Now, we didn't know how you wanted your furniture arranged. The missus can help move it where you like.

"Ralph, you and I and perhaps your oldest boy there need to go to the barn. You ought to learn our routine as soon as possible. One of my men is leaving tomorrow. He helps with the third-shift milking. You and your boy will replace him and his son."

Third shift would last until seven o'clock in the morning. Ben was tired from traveling and lack of sleep, but when Father urged him, "Let's go," he obeyed.

Esther didn't know where to begin. She wondered if Ralph and Ben had to go without supper and a night's rest. A knock at the door broke into her thoughts.

"Polly, *guck mol wer an die Dier is* (see once who's at the door)."

Mrs. Olson stepped inside with a steaming kettle of vegetable soup. She marched over to the stove and placed it on one of the burners.

"I'll turn this on low to keep it warm. The men will be back in about an hour." She stopped long enough to introduce herself. "Oh, yes, I'm Roberta Olson. I know what it's like to move. Everything's all a-clutter. So I told Mr. Olson I'm bringing in supper tonight and get you set up.

"There are still homemade rolls and a bowl of fruit in the car. Maybe your girl here could help me bring them in. Then we'll get acquainted."

"*Ya,*" agreed Mother as she nodded to Polly.

Shyly Polly followed Roberta Olson outside to her car.

"Polly, is it? My, what a pretty name. How old are you?"

"Eleven."

"Well, you're practically a lady!"

Polly felt important and eagerly helped carry the rest of the food into the kitchen.

Effie kept wandering to the large box of bedding. It was the first she left her mother's side since they had arrived.

"Now," planned Esther, "we might as well unpack the bedding first. I'll fix a floor bed for the baby. He should sleep now since he's had his bottle." She began to open the box with Mrs. Olson's help.

"What's in there?" asked Roberta.

"I don't know, but I heard something, too."

Gingerly they opened it, and there lay Spottie, the kitten, none the worse for traveling.

"My land! How did that kitty get in there?" Mrs. Olson wondered.

"*Ach* my, I don't know." Esther was embarrassed.

"I bet I know," Polly volunteered. "Effie put her in there."

"Did you, Effie?" her mother asked.

The little girl nodded. She held tightly to the hungry feline and kept saying, "My kitty."

"I don't know what to do with a kitten. We have no barn here," Esther told Roberta Olson.

"Oh, we have lots of cats at our dairy barn. I'll take her over there and feed her. Your daughter can come and play with her whenever she wants to."

Roberta helped Esther set up sleeping cots and unpack dishes. "Come on," she said, picking up Spottie. "Now that you have been let out of the bag, I'll take you home, you little stowaway. Bet you're hungry."

She laughed as she went out the door.

73

11

Lizards and Lectures

Esther was more than a little disappointed with their new home. The house was much smaller than the one she left behind. Nothing seemed right. Floors were uneven, and doors didn't close all the way.

There were so many new gadgets. She had never used an electric stove. How could one possibly cook without a flame? Mrs. Olson had shown her how to operate the stove, but she wasn't sure how long it would take for things to cook.

Just as Roberta had told them, Ralph and Ben returned to the house in an hour.

"Polly, you should see all those cows!" Ben exclaimed. "They don't milk them by hand, either. Machines do the milking."

"*Ach*, Ben, stop making up such stories. Anyone knows machines can't milk."

"It's true. Ask Dad, if you don't believe me."

"*Kummet esse* (come eat)," Mother called.

It didn't take the children long to find their places at the table.

"Let's give God thanks for a safe journey, for our food, and for work," Father said as he bowed his head in silent prayer.

Each family member did the same except Effie. She wiggled and whined.

"What's wrong with her?" Ralph asked his wife.

"She's tired, as we all are," Esther replied.

"*Ach,* she *gridles* (fusses) because Mrs. Olson took Spottie," Polly remarked.

"What are you talking about?" her dad wondered.

Mother wished Polly hadn't said anything, but it was too late now.

"Effie sneaked her kitten along in the box of bedding," Esther explained.

"All this way? I suppose it's dead, being shut up in that box so long," Ralph guessed.

"No," Polly answered. "It was a box made for oranges, with holes in it. Mrs. Olson took Spottie along to the barn. She said Effie can come and play with it anytime."

"No, she can't," Father declared. "I don't want her wandering over to the barns. Effie, *du bist en nixnutzich Meedel* (you're a naughty girl). Esther, I hope you punished her. We must train our children early in life. If we don't when they're young, what will they be when they get older?"

"*Ya,*" Esther answered. She looked at her young daughter with pity. It was hard enough on the older ones who knew why they came here. How much harder on a child who couldn't understand!

"This soup is good," Ralph commented. "Where did you get the fruit? How did you find time to bake these rolls?"

"Oh, I didn't. Mrs. Olson brought supper in. She said she knows what it's like to move."

"How nice the people are here!" Ralph remarked. "I expect we'll like it fine. Once we write to the home folks, it wouldn't surprise me if many of them move here, too."

"But what about the electricity, telephone, and bathroom. What will the church say? They were forbidden back home."

Polly held her breath, waiting for an answer.

"It's entirely different here," Father declared. "Back home, we owned our place, or at least we were buying it. Everything we had there, we bought. But here, these appliances don't belong to us. Therefore, the church will allow us to use them. I settled that with our ministers before we left."

Esther wished he had told her, but she remembered how busy he was getting everything organized. She was glad they could still be right with the church.

Polly and Ben were relieved to hear their dad explain that they could use these things. They would not have to cut them off or tear them out of the house, as they had heard of other Amish families doing who had bought houses from the *Englisch* (non-Amish).

"Bedtime," Ralph announced. "Mom, Effie, the baby, and I will take the large bedroom next to the bathroom. The rest of you will share the bedroom facing the road."

Polly didn't mind sharing a room with Sara. She was used to sharing a bed with her. But the boys in the same room! She did not like that at all.

"We don't have enough space for your own bedroom. Tomorrow I'll put up a dividing sheet for you," Mother promised.

The four older children got ready for bed in the dark. Mother and Father had cots to sleep on. The smaller children slept on floor beds made of comforters and quilts spread out for them. They were so tired, even the floor felt good.

"Ben," Polly whispered, "what was it like?"

"What was *what* like? You don't make sense."

"Mr. Olson's place — the barn and everything."

"There are lots of cows and a big chicken house. He has other people working for him, and he has children of his own."

"Does he have any girls?"

"I saw one about your size. Anyway, I think it was a girl."

"Don't you know?"

"They called her Rose Ann. She had long hair, but she dressed like *Englisch* boys do. I guess she's a girl though, 'cause she giggled a lot."

"I hope I get to see her."

"You will."

"How do you know?"

"Well, I heard her dad tell our dad that you could help his daughter feed the chickens and gather eggs. He said he would pay you."

Polly was delighted. "Oh, goody!" she exclaimed more loudly than she intended to. "I'll have a friend."

Father pounded against the wall and called a warning, "You children go to sleep. If I hear any more talking, I'm coming in there. *Es is net fer nix* (it won't be for nothing)."

The children knew what he meant. Silence reigned throughout the little house.

For a while, sleep eluded Polly. How lucky they were to have modern conveniences. No more trips to the outhouse in the dead of the night. She felt deliciously safe and snug.

Wait until her cousins read the letters she would write. Wouldn't they want to move to Texas, too?

Yes, Polly felt secure . . . until sometime after she drifted off to sleep. She awoke with a start to find something slithering across her arm. Screaming in terror, she aroused the entire family.

Mother and Father came swiftly. "*Was is letz* (what's wrong)?" Father asked.

"Something crawled across my arm."

"What did it look like?" Mother quizzed her.

"I don't know. It was dark in here."

"It's probably long gone," Father tried to calm her. "The way you screamed, you scared it off. Sure you weren't dreaming, were you? I don't see anything. Now go to sleep, and no more screaming, or the next time, if I have to come in here —"

"*Datt geht's* (there it goes)!" Ben exclaimed, pointing at a little green thing.

"*Ach*, that's just a lizard. He won't hurt you." Ralph caught him and tossed him outside.

Polly shivered. She hoped her bed would be set up soon. She certainly didn't care for lizards or lectures.

12

Barn-Paint Shoes

There was not much time for setting up beds and filling straw ticks. Chores seemed to last all day. Mr. Olson had field hands who took care of crops. Ralph and his family were assigned to the barns, to help with the dairy and chicken business.

Ben had never fed so many calves in his life, and Polly had never gathered so many eggs. There was a bright spot in Polly's work. She was with Rose Ann.

The very minute the girls met, Polly liked her. She looked just like a young Cinderella. Such beautiful long blond hair, tied with a blue ribbon! Rose Ann's sparkling blue eyes matched the color of her hair bow. She smiled, revealing a row of even pearly white teeth.

The only things that didn't fit the fairy tale were the shirt and overalls she wore. Polly pictured her in a gorgeous white gown with a blue sash.

Both girls were a bit shy at first. But by the end of the day, they were chattering like magpies.

"I think you're pretty," Polly remarked.

"Thank you," Rose Ann responded. "You're pretty, too, but why do you dress so funny-looking?"

"Mom says I have to. It's our way. She says plain and simple is best."

"Oh, I'll let you wear some of my clothes if you want to," Rose Ann offered.

"No, I wouldn't be allowed to dress like you do."

"Not in overalls. I mean, in one of my dresses. I have ever so many. I'd let you choose."

Polly relished the thought but knew her parents would never allow her to take the chance of even trying on those fancy dresses.

Each week Rose Ann and her mother stopped by before going shopping. Sometimes Esther went along for groceries. She had started a small kitchen garden, and since she baked bread, churned their own butter, and cut corners, they didn't have to buy much at the store.

Mr. Olson had given them a good guernsey cow for their own use. The milk she gave was nice and rich. Mother skimmed the cream from the top, and it made good butter and ice cream, which they now could keep in the refrigerator that came with the house. In addition to her pay, Polly was allowed to bring home all the cracked eggs they wanted.

Before long, Mr. Olson also cleared out a storage shed and fixed it for a makeshift barn for the Millers. This would be handy for keeping the guernsey and a horse. The surrey had arrived, and Ralph was looking for a driving horse to pull it.

Perhaps Effie was happiest of all, for now her kitten had a home with them again.

One day when Mrs. Olson came by, she had a favor to ask. "Mrs. Miller," she began, "could Rose Ann stay here while you and I go for groceries? She said she would rather play with Polly than go into town with us."

"That would be alright. They will have to play as quietly as possible. Ralph needs to get some sleep before third-shift milking."

"If it causes a problem, I'll take her along."

"No, no. I'll remind Polly. She's used to keeping the younger ones away from the bedroom while Ralph is sleeping."

"Well, if you're sure now."

"Yes, I'm sure. Levi and Effie are playing outside. Ben is also sleeping, and Baby William will take a nap."

"It won't take us as long if it's only the two of us," Mrs. Olson said.

Polly and Rose Ann were excited.

"You look like a picture-book girl," Polly told Rose Ann.

For the first time she saw her friend wearing a dress. It was a pink chiffon with a full skirt that billowed out like a fluffy cloud as she twirled round and round. Lace trim set off the round collar and cuffs. Such puffed sleeves! Polly was awestruck.

"You want to wear it?" Rose Ann asked, seeing Polly's wistfulness.

"Oh no, Miss, I couldn't!"

"We could trade. I'd like to see how it would be to switch."

Although Polly knew if caught she would deal with another kind of switch, she could resist no longer. "And your shoes. Could we trade shoes? I've always wanted white ones."

"Okay, let's," Rose Ann agreed.

"We'll go to the fruit cellar. No one will come down there."

Polly shivered with excitement more than from the cold. The basement was warmer, though, than some parts of the house.

"Take you hair down, Polly. Can you braid mine and put them up like yours?"

This had gone far enough. "If I take my hair down, my Mom will scold me. I can't put it up again."

"Well, at least, can you braid mine?" Rose

Ann begged. "I can't wear your little cap if you don't. I mean, it won't look right."

"I'll try, but I don't have any string to braid into it and tie it up."

Polly was good at braiding. She had first practiced on the fly harness for horses back in Ohio. Later, to Sara and Effie's sorrow, she practiced on them.

"You look beautiful," Rose Ann told Polly.

"Now *you* look funny," Polly laughed.

"Oh, I wish I could dress like this forever and ever!" Polly exclaimed. "If only we weren't Amish. If only I could have white shoes."

"Well, why can't you?" Rose Ann wondered. "Look, here are some pails of leftover paint my dad stored down here. If we can find white paint, we could paint your black shoes white. Here are some brushes. Dad painted our barn last summer, and I know we had paint left over."

Polly helped look at the color labels and paint stains on the containers. There was red, several colors of blue, brown, and an ugly gray.

"There it is," cried Rose Ann. "Now to pry the lid off." They worked and worked with a rusty old spike until the lid yielded to their efforts.

Without stirring the sluggish old paint and

without thinking of the consequences, the girls went to work.

"Now we'll leave them to dry."

And dry they did, to a stiff, uncomfortable sight.

"You can't wear white shoes with black shoe strings," Rose Ann said. "Here, let's dip them in the paint and hang them to dry."

The girls talked and playacted until they heard Baby William crying.

"We have to go now," Polly said. Quickly the girls changed back into their own garb.

"But what about my shoes?" Polly lamented. "I can't hide them! Oh, we shouldn't have done this."

After that episode, Ralph Miller forbade his daughters to play with Rose Ann. "You should have known better than let her stay here," he told his wife.

To Polly he said, "White stands for purity. Only the angels in heaven are pure. I'll remove that paint with turpentine, and you'll wear them as they are. Whoever heard of barn-paint shoes? If you pull such a stunt again, there'll be stiffer punishment."

However, Polly was done with white shoes.

13

Seven-Year Itch

For a while longer, Baby William was extra *gridlich* (fussy) with his colic.

"Can't you keep the *Bobbli* (baby) quiet so I can get some sleep?" Ralph asked Polly.

She had been playing with him all forenoon. He fussed when she rocked him. Even when she offered him a bottle of milk, he squirmed and whined.

"How is a man supposed to work third shift if he can't get his sleep?"

Polly felt as though it were her fault, although she couldn't imagine why.

"Polly," Mother called, "bring *es Bobbli* (the baby) out here in the kitchen. It's not so close to the *Bettkammer* (bedroom). Maybe Dad won't hear him cry then."

Polly's arms ached, but obediently she hiked him on her hip and lugged William to the kitchen.

"Mom, what are those red things on the baby's neck?"

"Where? Let me see." Esther took the baby and examined him further. "*Ach du lieber* (oh my land)! This looks to me like the seven-year itch. Where could he have picked up something like this?"

"I've got a red rash on my stomach that itches awful at times," Polly complained. "Rose Ann told me it's probably from the dust in the chicken house, and that when I get used to the dust, the rash will go away."

Esther checked Polly. "You've got it, too. I bet Ben and Effie have it. They have been so cranky lately. I figured it was because they were homesick, but now I wonder. You children sat on those old fallen logs back by the cattle shoot, didn't you?"

"Yes, Mom. We watched them load some cows on the big truck."

"Sometimes mites are on old wood, and if they get under your skin, you break out with an itchy rash."

"Why do they call it seven-year itch?" Polly asked. "Does it last that long?"

"Not if you treat it. The itch is so hard to get rid of and so uncomfortable that it seems like seven years before it's gone. Well, I'll just have to boil all our clothes and lay out in the sun the things that can't be boiled.

"We need to fix a sulfur-and-lard ointment to treat ourselves. Even though some of us don't have the rash, we'll all use the ointment. We must make sure we're safe. It's very catching and spreads quickly. *Ach,* I do hope the sulfur *Schmier* (salve) is not too harsh for the *Bobbli* (baby)."

Esther's workload was doubled now. She boiled and washed and washed and boiled some more. She was thankful for a bathroom. Back home in Ohio, she would have needed to bring the old tin tub into the kitchen and heat gallons of water to bathe her family.

Two days into the treatment, the washer broke down. Esther was hanging freshly laundered clothes on the line. Polly was putting another batch through the wringer when she first noticed the problem. Small blue streaks of acrid smoke spiraled up from the washer. It smelled almost as bad as the sulfur salve they had to use.

Dropping everything, Polly ran out to tell her mother. "*Es schtinke* (it stinks)!"

"What stinks? What are you talking about?"

"The washing machine. It makes smoke."

Esther left the basket of clothes and followed her daughter to the house. The room was filled with smoke. It stung their eyes and burned their throat. The washer had stopped.

"*Ach* my! I don't know what to do," Esther

groaned. "If this were the gasoline washer I had in Ohio, maybe it wouldn't have happened." But she didn't want to complain, since she believed that all things God permitted to befall her were for her good.

"I don't want to wake your father," she told Polly. "He worked overtime, and it was late when he came home this morning. Keep that door open so the smoke will clear out."

She was glad Effie and Levi were outside playing and Ben was taking a nap. He, too, worked from eleven at night to seven or later in the morning. Ben liked dairy work, but he didn't care for the graveyard shift. It was hard getting used to daytime sleeping. Once he started to school, it became quite difficult.

"What's going on out here?" Ralph asked, rubbing his eyes. "My eyes are stinging from smoke. It's good I woke up! Why didn't you unplug the machine?" Ralph realized at once where the smoke came from.

"I don't know anything about these electric contraptions," Esther reminded him.

"The motor must have burned out," her husband decided.

"*Wie in die Welt* (how in the world) am I going to do all the washing?"

"You have a scrub board, don't you? I guess that's what you'll have to use until we get another washer."

Esther did not comment. She dreaded the thought of using a scrub board. Polly felt sorry for her mother, and she also knew that she would be expected to share a part of that task.

By evening Polly's tender hands were blistered from wringing out article after article of clothing. Her knuckles were skinned and raw from taking her turn at the scrub board. She felt like complaining, but then she saw her mother's bleeding fingers and her bent frame as she tried to straighten from bending over the scrub board so long.

Polly wondered again why they had to move to Texas. Few letters had been received in the months since the Millers left Ohio. One brought the good news that Sylvanus Yoders and Noah Yutzys were moving to Texas. More Amish families were considering it.

The other letter was from Amos Beachys, who had rented the Miller farm. It informed Ralph and Esther that all was going well. However, they were sorry to report that Buster, their dog, had died. It happened about a month after the Millers left.

"We think he grieved himself to death," Amos wrote. This indeed was sad news for the children.

"No use *brutzing* (pouting). It was just a dog," Ralph told his children.

They didn't like their dad's comment.

"It was *not* just a dog," Ben told Polly that night. "It was *our* dog."

"*Ya,* it was our Buster," she agreed.

The next day, something happened that lifted Polly's spirits. Mr. Olson and Ralph brought a new washer out to the house.

"Mom," declared Polly, "I don't think I could have scrubbed one more piece of clothing. That seven-year itch seemed more like seventeen years."

"Well, it's all gone now. Just stay away from old fallen logs."

"For sure I will," Polly promised.

14

Grummbiere Mush

Time passed swiftly for the Miller family living at Lone Prairie, Texas. In the next several years, nine other families settled in the same area. They had formed a small church, meeting in homes every second Sunday.

Most of the families who moved in were younger parents with small children. Thus, there was little social life for the few teenagers.

Ralph had made two trips back to Ohio to check on his farm and encourage others to move to Texas. Late one fall, he was planning to take along his wife and the younger children to visit *Freindschaft* (relatives) and friends back in the home community.

"Can't we all go?" Esther asked wistfully.

"I should say not. It costs enough as it is, without dragging all the children along," her husband insisted.

"Perhaps I shouldn't go then."

"Your parents wouldn't let me hear the last

of it if I didn't bring you. In fact, your mother made me feel guilty the last time I went alone. I declare, she acts as if I were mean to my family. I'm only trying to get our farm paid off so we can all go home for good. I have to cut corners wherever I can."

"I know, Ralph. You're doing fine, too. It's just that it seems so long."

"It should only be a year or two yet if all goes well." Ralph was pleased that Esther approved of how he was managing their finances. The farm payoff schedule was steep, but when they had it paid off, they would be in a better position to help their children get started on farms for themselves.

The older children wanted to go back, but they would surely miss the modern conveniences to which they had grown accustomed. William and Effie hadn't been old enough when they moved to remember their Ohio home. Levi had only vague memories, and Sara's were a little sharper.

Polly and Ben, however, often longed to return to their cousins and friends. In the few letters they received from home, there was news of *Rumschpringe* time (going out with the young folks). Boys of Polly's age were getting buggies of their own.

"Ben," remarked Polly one day, "if we were living at our old home, I would soon be going to Sunday night singing. I'm almost sixteen and old enough for *Rumschpringe,* but what chance do I have out here?"

"I know," answered Ben. "There aren't enough *Yunge* (young folks) here at Lone Prairie to have singings. It seems that all we do is work, work, work!"

"I agree. And when we aren't working, we're so tired we fall asleep."

"Well, I heard Dad say that maybe in a year or two, he'll have the home place paid off. Then we can move back."

"*Ach,* I've heard him say that before," Polly griped. "Do you think it will really happen this time?"

"Guess we'll just have to wait and see."

"Children," their dad announced at the dinner table, "I bought tickets for Mom, me, William, and Effie, to take a trip back to Ohio next week. The rest of you are old enough to look after things while we're gone.

"Mr. Olson has hired a boy from town to take my place while I'm gone. His name is Tom Dawson. He'll need a place to stay because it's a good ways from his home. I told him he could board here for two weeks. Polly, you know how to cook well enough to feed a hired hand. He can use our bedroom."

Esther looked startled. She knew nothing of this plan. "But, Ralph," she objected, "we don't even know this boy. Are you sure we can trust him?"

"Do you think Mr. Olson would hire someone who couldn't be trusted?" Ralph had a slight frown on his face.

Esther did not answer. She knew her husband's mind was made up.

Levi was old enough now that he helped around the dairy. His work was feeding calves and washing milk equipment. Ben helped with the actual milking operations.

On the morning they left for Ohio, Esther gave her children last-minute instructions. "Be sure you don't forget to lock the doors at night and while you're at school or work. We're living among the *Englisch,* and this is a rented house, so we have to take care of it.

"If it turns cold, bring my potted flower plants in. Don't leave any lights burning during the night, and read your Bible everyday."

"Come on, Esther, or we'll miss our train," Ralph called. "Mr. Olson is waiting to drive us to the train station."

Esther reluctantly gave tearful good-byes to Polly, Ben, and Levi, and then followed her husband to the car. William, Effie, and Sara were already seated in the back.

Sara couldn't believe that she was going. Lately she'd been helping with the gathering of eggs and a few other chores with the chickens. At the last minute, Ralph said they would take her along.

Since she was ten, she could help watch the youngest two. Sara was too thrilled about the trip to complain about that responsibility.

Polly liked Tom Dawson the minute he walked into the house. He had dark curly hair, steel-gray eyes, and the friendliest smile she had ever seen. She judged him to be about eighteen years old. He held a big cowboy hat in his hands. Slowly he twirled the hat around as he spoke.

"Well, ma'am," he drawled in that southern accent, "I guess this is where I get my grub."

"Gr-gr-grub?" stammered Polly, her face blushing a pretty pink.

"Oh, I mean, I was told I could eat here."

"*Ya* — I mean yes." How Polly wished she would have combed her hair and put on her blue dress. That was the prettiest-color dress she owned.

Now here she was, wearing her ugly old faded brown one. She had grown to be an attractive young lady. Her hair was a cornsilk blond, and her eyes as blue as the summer sky. The peaches-and-cream complexion was unmarred by makeup.

She's beautiful, thought Tom as they stood there. Tom sensed that radiating from her

was something mysterious, childlike inno-
cence with no pretense.

"Where do I wash up?" he asked.

"Oh, yes!" Polly felt a bit foolish that he had
to ask for directions. "Right in there." She
pointed him toward the bathroom.

Ben came whistling through the kitchen
door. "Tom here yet?" he asked.

"Who?" asked Polly.

"Tom, the boy that's taking Dad's place
while he's gone."

"Yes, he's washing up in the bathroom."

"What's wrong with you?" Ben wondered.
"Your face is pink, and you look like you're in
some other world. Why isn't dinner on?"

"*Ach*, I'll get it right away." Polly pushed
her *Kapp* (head cap for Amish women and
girls) back on her head so more of her hair
would show and smoothed her apron. She began ladling food from kettles on the stove into
serving bowls.

Tom made his way to the kitchen, still
holding that big hat.

"Hang your hat there on a wall peg," Ben
told him as he waved toward the wall. "I'll
wash up, and then we can eat."

"Smells mighty good," Tom commented.

"What did you fix?" Ben asked Polly.

"*Grummbiere* mush — *ach*, I mean mashed
potatoes, meat, gravy, and *Pasching* —

peaches." Polly was still flustered.

The children bowed their heads in silent prayer, giving thanks for food as they had been taught.

Tom just waited for his *Grummbiere* mush.

15

If Only!

Polly and Rose Ann had some exciting plans. Now that her parents were gone, Polly decided to have Rose Ann spend Sunday afternoon with her. Since they were older, they worked in the packing house, candling and boxing eggs for shipping.

Polly liked that better than working among the smelly, noisy, pecking hens. However, this change gave her and Rose Ann little time to talk. The packing house was closed on Sunday, so they had all day for other things.

"Be sure to come right after lunch," Polly told Rose Ann.

"What if your dad finds out?" Rose Ann asked. "Remember, he said I was not to come over there anymore. Why doesn't he want me to come and visit you?" She seemed bewildered.

"Oh, he didn't like it that I wanted white shoes. He thinks if we're together too much, I will want to dress like you and be *englisch*."

"Well, do you?" Rose Ann asked.

"Oh, yes, but I don't know if it's right."

"Well, why wouldn't it be right?"

"Dad says it's worldly, and if I were to dress that way, I'd be proud. He says the Bible tells us that pride goes before a fall, and it's a sin to be proud."

"Doesn't he like for you to have nice things? You're so beautiful, I should think he would want you to dress in pretty, bright clothes."

"No, he says we're to be different."

"But why?" her friend persisted.

"I don't know, but we won't think about that now. We don't have church this Sunday, so we'll have more free time. You just come then."

"Oh, I will," Rose Ann promised. "I'll bring one of my dresses for you to wear, and maybe we can fix your hair different."

"Oh, Rose Ann, that would be fun. But my parents must never know. Maybe we'd better not do it. Ben or Levi might see me and tattle."

"We'll watch out for them. Anyhow, won't they be napping, or outside playing, or choring in the barn?"

"Oh, I guess it will work out fine then."

The girls eagerly awaited the arrival of Sunday and the dress-up experiment.

Since Polly was almost sixteen, she was no longer going to school. She was a good student. After she finished the eighth grade, instead of going to high school, she had stayed in the one-room country school. Until she was old enough to quit school, she helped the teacher with the younger children and read most of the books in the library.

Polly had learned her lessons well. She loved books and was an excellent reader. Magazines and books were scarce in the Miller home. Her dad felt the Bible, the *Farm Journal*, and their textbooks from school were sufficient. Polly often read to her younger siblings from the school readers, but her dad did not approve of many of those stories.

"Fairy tales," he declared, "fill their heads full of stuff which isn't true. Why can't they use readers like we used to?"

To avoid the hassle, Polly made it a point not to read within hearing distance of her father anymore. Besides, Sara and Effie seldom brought their readers home since Ralph had voiced his opinion.

The first Sunday after their parents were gone, Tom Dawson had gone home for the day. So Polly made a quick, simple lunch for Ben, Levi, and herself.

"What are you going to do this afternoon, Ben?" Polly asked.

"I'm going to catch up on some sleep," he replied. "Don't you make noise, either."

Now he sounds like Dad, Polly thought.

"And what about you, Levi?" Polly wondered.

"I'm going fishing, and I'll be back in time for supper."

Ben finished lunch and went to his bedroom for a long nap. Levi dug a few worms and took off for the stream with his fishing rod and a bucket to bring back any fish he caught.

Polly had washed the dishes and just put the last plate in the cupboard when she heard a knock. She opened the door, and there stood Rose Ann, carrying a big brown bag.

"Are we all alone?"

"Levi's gone fishing. But Ben is here, sleeping in his bedroom."

"I wish we were alone. Look what I brought." Rose Ann opened the bag for Polly to see.

"Oh, Rose Ann!" Polly saw a pretty green dress, some white shoes, and a few things she couldn't identify.

"Let's close the kitchen door so Ben can't hear us," Rose Ann suggested.

Quickly Polly obliged. Rose Ann deposited the contents of the bag on the kitchen table.

"Now let's dress you up. Here, I'll help you with the dress."

Polly was old enough that she dressed in the garb of the older girls. Her clothes were fastened with straight pins, and her hair was no longer braided. She put it up by herself now in a neat bun at the nape of her neck.

"Oh, the dress fits you perfectly. Now put on these bobby socks and the white shoes. Let your hair down. Here, I'll brush it for you. I have a brush.

"You need some makeup. Hold still while I put a little lipstick on you. A bit of blue eye shadow will be perfect," Rose Ann recommended.

She had taken full charge. It all happened so fast, Polly felt faint.

"Take a look at yourself in that mirror above the sink. It's a shame it's cracked, but you can get an idea. Polly, you *are* beautiful!"

Just then they heard someone step into the kitchen from outside. Rose Ann and Polly turned around, startled. There stood Tom Dawson, who had come back early.

"Polly, is it really you?" Tom asked.

"Yes, it's Polly alright," Rose Ann announced, beaming.

"You should always dress like that!" Tom declared with appreciation.

If only Tom wouldn't have come early! If only she hadn't dressed this way. Oh, if only . . . but it was too late!

16

The Rodeo

Polly quickly made her way to her bedroom, where she changed into her own clothes. Smoothing her hair and putting it back into a bun, she reentered the kitchen.

"Here, Rose Ann," she offered, handing the bag with the green dress to her friend.

"Oh, you keep it. I have ever so many, and you look so nice in it."

"No, I couldn't."

"Well, why not?"

"It's against our church rules."

"Why don't you keep it?" Tom urged. "If you dress like that this coming Sunday, I'll take you to the rodeo."

"What's a rodeo?" Polly asked.

"It's horseback riding, calf roping, and things like that. You would love it. Your brother Ben told me he wanted to go. Why don't we all go together?"

Polly hesitated. "I don't think so."

"Why ever not?" Tom wondered.

"For one thing, Mom and Dad wouldn't like it, and we can't leave Levi here alone."

"Your mom and dad need not know. They're hundreds of miles away. And Levi always wants to go fishing. We can just tell him we're going to town to look around while he fishes."

"Ben and Tom and you and I can go," urged Rose Ann. Please say you will, Polly. You'll have fun. I know you will!"

To her own amazement, Polly found herself saying, "Okay, if Ben goes, I will."

Ben was eager to accept the invitation. He loved horses and excitement.

After Tom and Rose Ann left, Polly had some doubts about Ben's approval if she dressed *englisch*. "Do you think I'll be eternally lost if I dress in Rose Ann's clothes and leave my hair hang free?" she asked her brother.

"No, I don't think so. Anyway, it will just be this once. And it's not like you're a member of the church already, pledged to keep all the church rules."

"Let's just tell Levi that Tom and Rose Ann asked us to go into town with them. He probably won't question us because he will be too *froh* (glad) to go fishing."

"That's true," Ben agreed. "We don't have many chances to be with young folks our age.

Nobody can blame us for wanting to get out once."

That is how it all started. With their parents gone, they didn't go to church the next Sunday. That afternoon found Ben rested from his chores on the night shift and eager to go.

Polly had mixed feelings. Now she wished she had not agreed to the scheme. She felt especially guilty as she read her Bible passage for the day. It was chapter six of the book of Ephesians. The first three verses especially convicted her:

"Children, obey your parents in the Lord, for this is right. Honor your father and mother, which is the first commandment with a promise, that it may be well with you and you might live long on the earth."

Polly wondered if her life might perhaps be shortened if she disobeyed. She decided to talk it over with Ben after Levi left to fish.

"Ben," she began, "I don't know if I should go. It makes me feel all *schiddlich* (shaky)."

"You promised you would go if I and Tom bought tickets for four. We can't back out now. *Was misse er denke* (what would he think)? He was kind enough to spend money to pay our way in. Who would Rose Ann be with if you don't go? I sure don't want her hanging around me and Tom."

Polly didn't have an answer for all Ben's arguments, so she began to get ready.

Tom picked up Rose Ann on the way to the Millers, and then the four of them were on their way.

"Oh, Polly, you look so nice," Rose Ann gushed. "I don't see how you can ever go back to wearing those plain, simple old clothes. Don't you think your parents would let you dress like this if they saw how different you look?"

"Goodness, no!"

"Well, we will just enjoy today," Rose Ann declared.

Polly didn't think she could, what with such a guilty conscience.

"Here we are," Tom announced, steering his car into the parking area. "Come on, let's go." They got out of the car.

Tom seemed to know his way around, and a lot of folks spoke to him as they joined the crowd.

"How many?" asked the man at the ticket stand.

"Four," Tom answered, "but I got tickets in advance. They are reserved seats, second row, middle section."

"Go right on in then, Tom. I gather you're not riding today."

"No, not this time, Al."

Ben was almost speechless. "Tom," he gasped, "you mean you ride in the rodeo?"

"Oh, once in a while," Tom admitted with a casual air. "You sit with Rose Ann, Ben. I want to sit with your sister."

That didn't please Ben, but he sat next to Rose Ann anyway. Tom was a pretty big man in Ben's eyes, and he didn't want to displease him.

Soon the action of the rodeo began. The first event was bareback riding. First out of the chute was a horse called Black Vapor. He was kicking and jumping the minute the gate opened.

Polly and Ben had never seen anything like it. They were both on the edge of their seats. Tom grinned at their excitement.

"Aren't you enjoying this?" Tom asked Polly.

"*Ach,* my! He'll get killed," she exclaimed.

"Oh, I doubt it. He knows how to ride."

The rider went the full time and was given a score of eighty-seven. All the other bareback riders had to either match or beat that score in order to win any big money.

"I can't see how they can stay on at all," Ben commented.

"If you think this is rough, wait till the bull-riding contest begins," Rose Ann bragged.

"What?" Ben exclaimed. "They do that too?"

Tom and Rose Ann laughed at the shock their young guests expressed.

Polly became so engrossed in the activities that she didn't even feel guilty anymore. Several times a rider was gored by a bull, but none seriously.

"Those clowns do a good job of protecting the riders, but I sure wouldn't want their job," Ben told Polly.

"That's it," stated Tom as the winner of each event was announced. "Guess we'd better go. I hope this won't be the last time we can do this. Did you enjoy it?"

Both Polly and Ben admitted they did.

Later, when they were alone, Polly commented, "*Ach,* Ben, the way those riders *blutzed* (bounced) around, it must hurt most *wunderbaar* (wonderful, terribly)."

17

Mixed Feelings

The rodeo was only the first of many times Polly and Tom met secretly. When Ralph Millers returned from their trip to Ohio, Tom was no longer needed in the dairy.

As Tom walked through the kitchen after picking up his belongings, he slipped a note to Polly. She quickly put it in her dress pocket, smoothing her apron over it.

Polly could hardly wait to find out what the note said. She made her way to the bathroom and took the folded paper from her pocket. "Meet me at the crossroad beyond your place Saturday night at nine. I'll watch for you." That was all Tom wrote.

Polly's heart was racing. She wondered what he wanted. By nine the family would be in bed — all except her dad and Ben. They had been moved to second shift since Ralph came back from Ohio. That meant that, starting this very day, they went to work at three in the afternoon and were on duty until eleven-thirty. That suited Ralph and Ben better.

"Now maybe we can get our rest, Ben," Ralph commented.

"I hope so," his son agreed.

Polly wondered if she should accept Tom's invitation to meet him Saturday night. Now she was grateful for the extra room that Mr. Olson had added onto the house soon after they had moved to Texas. Since then, the boys were in a bedroom of their own.

But how could she leave without Sara or Effie hearing her? *No need to worry about it now. Maybe I won't even go,* she thought.

Ralph and Esther were flooded with questions from Ben, Polly, and Levi.

"Does our place still look the same? Did you see cousins Ada and Rachel? How big are they?" Polly asked.

"Does cousin Freddie have his own rig yet?" queried Ben. "He wrote in his last letter that he might get one soon."

"Did Amos Beachys get another dog to take Buster's place?" Levi wanted to know.

"Is Ervin Shetler *rumschpringing* yet (going with the young folks)?" questioned Ben.

"Are cousin Fannie and her mom and dad moving out here? Fannie said they might," Polly wondered hopefully.

"How do you children expect us to eat

while you ask so many questions?" their dad objected. They were eating Saturday lunch, and everyone was at the table. There was no school for the younger ones, and Ben and Ralph didn't go to the dairy till three o'clock.

"We'll answer your questions later," Mother declared.

The children wondered how much later. They finished their meal in silence.

That evening twilight stole softly across the Texas prairie. There was a full moon which seemed to hang from the sky, flooding the world with its light.

"Children, get your baths. It will soon be bedtime," Esther reminded them.

Her mind went back to Saturday nights in Ohio and their old home. She was ever so grateful for a real bathtub instead of the old tin washtub. No more water to carry or heat to take baths. No more tub to empty.

Yet Esther missed her Ohio home. She missed her big house, her beautiful flower beds, the large lawn, her many friends, but especially her relatives and the church. The one comfort she had was that Ralph promised to go back — someday.

While Esther was dwelling on these things, her daughter was entertaining thoughts of her own. Should she go to the crossroad to meet Tom? She felt both excited and wicked.

Finally she decided, *If everyone is in bed and Sara and Effie are asleep by nine, I'll go.* That would be the sign she would look for.

"Come on, Sara. You and Effie hurry and get to bed," Polly told her sisters.

"But I'm not sleepy yet," Sara objected.

"You heard what Mom said. You have had your bath. Now go to bed."

Esther was grateful for Polly's help. "*Du bist un grosse Hilf* (you are a big help)," she praised her. "I'm still so tired from our trip, and I'm ready for bed."

The words of appreciation brought more guilt for Polly. Her mother didn't realize why she was trying to hurry her siblings to bed.

"Tell us a story," Effie coaxed.

"*Ya,* do. We'll go to sleep sooner if you do," Sara promised.

"Well, alright, but just one," Polly agreed.

Both girls jumped into bed while Polly sat on a straight-back chair. She was glad she had a half-bed to herself. Since her brothers moved out, the room was less crowded and much more private.

"Now," she began, "I'll tell you the story of Cinderella if you don't tell anyone."

"Not even Dad and Mom?" asked Effie.

"Especially not Dad and Mom!"

"Why not?" Effie wondered.

"Because it's a fairy tale, and they don't like fairy tales."

"Why?"

"Because it's only a make-believe story. They believe we should only tell things that are true. Now, do you want to hear it or not?" Polly was exasperated.

"*Ya*, I do," Effie answered.

"Then be quiet and listen." Polly launched into a vivid and glowing report of the life of Cinderella.

Several times the girls sat up in rapt awe, but by the time Cinderella was just ready to live happily ever after, two girls were getting sleepy. No doubt their dreams were of pretty girls, pink and white gowns, and a carriage drawn by prancing horses.

Polly turned the light switch off, but the room was bathed in moonlight. She slipped into her own bed and waited. By and by she heard the even breathing of her sisters.

Her own heart was pounding so hard that she wondered if someone might hear it. Then the clock on the kitchen shelf struck nine. Quietly Polly stepped to her closet, took the green dress from its hiding place, and got ready. She always slept with her hair loosened, so that was already taken care of. Carrying her shoes, she stole noiselessly out the back door.

What does Tom want to see me about? Polly hurried to the crossroad. She knew she was a bit late. Perhaps Tom had been there and left, thinking she wasn't coming. Then she saw it. A car parked by the roadside. She was glad for the brightness of the moon.

Polly saw Tom step from his car and come to meet her. "I'm so glad you came," he enthused.

Polly still had mixed feelings, but she certainly found this exciting!

18

At the Crossroad

"What do you want, Tom?" Polly asked as soon as they were seated in his car.

"I wanted to see you again, Polly."

"Why?"

"Do I need a reason? I just wanted to talk and see if you would like to come to the rodeo with me again sometime."

"Oh, Ben and I would like that, but I don't think Dad would let us."

"Where did you get the idea that I want Ben to go along? Oh, well, it would be fine if Ben can come." *In fact,* Tom reasoned, *that may be the only way Ralph would let his daughter go.*

"Why wouldn't your dad let you go with me?" Tom asked. "I've never done him any harm."

"But you're an *Englischer,*" Polly explained.

"Is that bad?"

"My dad thinks so. Well, he thinks we

should only be with Amish people because we were born Amish."

"Then maybe I should only be friends with Catholics, because I was born Catholic."

"*Ach,* I don't know. I'm so mixed up," Polly remarked. *What am I doing here anyway? If I have to sneak out, does that mean it isn't right?*

"Let's not just sit here wasting time," Tom declared. "Where would you like to go?"

"I don't know any places around here. You choose."

"How about Bill's Bar-B-Que? We could get us a bite to eat. Are you hungry?"

"No, not really."

"In that case, we will just get some ice cream."

That sounded tempting to Polly. Tom started his car and eased it slowly onto the roadway.

"I'll have to be home by eleven," Polly told Tom.

"Why? Are you afraid your lovely green dress will turn back to your drab Amish one and my car will become a pumpkin?"

"What?" She thought it sounded much like her favorite girlhood fairy tale.

"I'm just teasing," Tom told her. "Don't worry, Cinderella, I'll have you home on time."

The Bar-B-Que grill was a noisy, smoke-filled place. It was filled with painted, silly girls and rough-looking cowboys.

"Hey, Tom, who's the girl?" one fellow shouted.

"She's a friend, and I respect her," Tom answered.

"Okay, okay. I was just asking."

Tom ordered two dishes of ice cream.

Polly felt ill at ease. "Let's get out of this place," she told Tom.

"Don't you want your ice cream?" he asked.

"Yes, but I don't care to eat it in here. Everyone is staring at me."

"Maybe that's because they don't often see such a naturally pretty girl."

This embarrassed Polly all the more.

"Okay, come on. We can eat our ice cream in the car," Tom agreed.

She followed him outside. The juke box was playing "The Yellow Rose of Texas," and they could hear it all the way to Tom's car. He held the door for Polly, and his friendly face beamed with pleasure. That smile warmed her heart. What was it about this boy that was so different from any she had met before?

"I'm sorry you aren't enjoying the evening," Tom apologized.

"Oh, I'm enjoying being with you," Polly

told him. "It's just that, when we were in that place, the Bar . . ." she hesitated.

"You mean the Bar-B-Que?"

"Yes, that's it. I didn't like that place at all. Let's not go there again."

"I promise we won't if you don't want to."

Two things made Tom happy. Polly had indicated she enjoyed his company, and since she asked him not to take her to the Bar-B-Que anymore, he assumed she planned to go with him again.

"I'm glad to hear you enjoy being with me, and I guess you're willing to go out some more with me since you asked me never to take you to the Bar-B-Que?"

It dawned on Polly what she had said. However, she had not meant to be so bold.

"Oh, Tom, I didn't mean it that way," Polly gasped.

"How did you mean it?"

"I don't know. Tom, I don't know if I can go with you again."

"I'm sorry to hear you say that. Polly, I've been thinking of signing up for rodeo riding, and I wanted you to come to bring me good luck."

"We don't believe in luck. But I'd like to come to the rodeo again," she added. "Tom, what if you'd get hurt riding one of those wild horses?"

"Would it matter to you if I did?"

"Of course it would. It matters if anyone gets hurt."

"If you don't believe in luck, what do you believe in?" Tom asked.

"Our parents say we must only believe what the Bible says. It's God's Word, you know."

"Well, I guess that advice is as good as you can get. Now as for riding wild horses, I won't do that."

Polly gave a slight sigh of relief.

"No," Tom continued, "I've decided to go in for bull riding."

"That's even worse!" Polly exclaimed. She forgot and her native tongue burst forth with "*Ach, mei Hatz* (oh, my heart)!"

"Don't look so shocked," Tom laughed. "You need not swear. I know what I'm doing."

"Oh dear, I wasn't swearing! I only forgot and used our language."

"Will you come if I sign up? You and Ben?"

"Ben can't come because now he works second shift. I almost forgot."

That suited Tom if now Polly would come alone.

"How can I come?" she asked. "The rodeo is Sunday afternoons, and Mom would ask where I'm going."

"Can't you tell her you're going to Rose

Ann's or for a walk?"

"Sara and Effie always tag along on walks. Maybe we'd better forget it."

"No," Tom declared. "We'll work out something."

"You'd better take me home now," Polly urged.

"Alright, Cinderella," Tom teased again.

"Drop me off by the crossroad, and I'll walk on home."

"I'd gladly drive you to your house," Tom offered.

"No, I can walk. It's best this way."

"When can I see you again?"

"I don't know."

"Look, every Tuesday I'll leave a note by the signpost at the crossroad. Look for them and answer."

Polly was already out of the car.

"Alright," she promised as she waved and started for home.

At the crossroad — that's our secret place, she said to herself.

19

The Rattler

"Mom, tell us again about your trip back home," coaxed Levi.

"*Ya,* tell us," Polly and Ben chimed, almost in unison.

"*Ach,* how many times must I tell you and answer your questions again?" Esther complained, half in fun.

"Well, we like to hear it because it seems so long since we lived there," Ben told her.

"I know," Esther agreed. "You miss our old home, too. So do I. Father said the farm is almost paid off, and maybe we can move back soon."

"I'm glad I got the day off from helping load those cattle so I can hear it all over again." Ben was enthusiastic.

"Well," started Mother, "*wo fange mir aa* (now where do we begin)?"

"With me," Levi suggested. "What I want to know is, did Amos' get another dog?"

"You know they did. In fact, he looks a lot like Buster did," Mother reported.

"But I bet he isn't as good or smart as Buster was," Levi insisted.

"I don't know about that. He must be a good watchdog, though, for he sure did *gautz* (bark) when we got there."

"Did you get to see cousin Ada and Rachel?" Polly wondered.

"I told you I saw Rachel but not Ada. I must say, Rachel has sure grown. She is a young woman now and has an *Alder* (boyfriend)."

"Really!" exclaimed Polly. "Who is it?"

"A boy from Pennsylvania. I think they said his name is Sam Troyer."

"I wonder how they met," Polly put in.

"Well, I can't tell you, for I don't know, but Sam Troyer is a good, solid Amish name, so I suppose she can't go wrong."

Polly felt a twinge of guilt. Did her mother suspect anything? She had destroyed all the notes Tom had left at their secret place, so her mother could not have found one of them.

"By the way, Polly," Mother continued, "Rachel asked about you. She said to say 'hello' and that you should write."

Ben asked about his cousins Freddie and Ervin Eash again.

"I don't know if Freddie has his own rig yet

or not, but yes, Ervin Eash is starting his *Rumschpringe*. I'm sorry to say he is acting rather wild. I feel so sorry for his parents.

"That's one thing I thank God for, our *gehorsam* (obedient) children," Esther told them. "I'm glad I can count on you to live true to the church."

Polly was smitten. *I must never go out with Tom Dawson again,* she thought. *What if Mom and Dad find out about my secret excursions?*

However, the next time she found a note at the crossroad hiding place, she changed her mind. *Maybe just one more time. I do need friends my own age.*

One time led to the next, and another year slipped by. Then one day she found a special message.

"Be sure to meet me on Saturday night no later than nine-fifteen," Tom wrote. "I have something very important to talk about. Please, please come. I'll be waiting. With love, Tom."

Polly shivered as she tore the note into tiny bits. No one had ever used the word *love* to her before. The letters she received from relatives or friends back home always ended with "your friend" or "cousin," whoever they might be, but never with "love."

Polly was sure her parents cared for her by what they did. But she knew it just wasn't the

Amish way for them to tell her they loved her.

Saturday night found Polly carefully sneaking out once more. It seemed as if every floorboard in the house creaked loudly with each step. Finally she reached the door and slipped quickly outside.

Polly noticed Mother's bedroom lamp was still burning. *Why,* she wondered, *isn't Mother in bed? Had she heard the creaking of the floor boards and was going to investigate?*

Polly did not know that her mother was kneeling by her bed, deeply in prayer for her family. Esther had never felt comfortable about their move west. Something didn't seem right, and she prayed much.

The children were growing up so fast, and Esther knew they needed friends. She counted it important that they have Christian boys and girls to associate with.

Some of the Amish families who came to Texas had moved back to their original homes again, for just that reason. She sincerely hoped that her family would do the same before long.

Polly found Tom impatiently waiting for her, leaning against the car. He opened the door on the passenger side and took her arm as she stepped inside. Then, making his way to the other side, he announced, "Tonight we're going down to Silver Lake.

"It's beautiful down there. I've been wanting to take you ever since we've been seeing each other. But I decided to wait for just the right time. Tonight's that time." He flashed her that big smile, and she basked in its glow.

"What did you want to talk to me about?" Polly asked.

"Oh, that will have to wait until we get to the lake. I don't want anything to spoil this night."

Polly wondered what in the world it might be, but she decided to enjoy the ride and wait.

"Don't forget," she told Tom, "you have to take me home before midnight."

"Yes, Cinderella," he laughed. "Don't worry about it."

The lake was magnificent, just as Tom had told her, with the water shimmering and shining in the moonlight. A few trees helped to frame the setting, and overhead was the big Texas star-studded sky.

"No wonder it's called Silver Lake." Polly gazed in awe. "It's beautiful!"

"I'm glad you like it." Tom was leaning toward her. "But it's not as beautiful as you are, my Cinderella."

Polly edged toward the door on her side. Tom was acting strangely, and there was a funny smell on his breath.

"Don't be so shy." He reached out and put

his arm around her shoulders. "Polly, I love you. I brought you here to ask you to marry me. We'll go to the justice of the peace tonight. Here, I've got the ring and everything. Please say yes."

Tom showed her a glittering ring. Reaching under the seat with his left hand, he produced a bottle. He turned his smile on even brighter and announced, "Look, I even remembered to bring wine to celebrate."

Polly was shocked. The smile that before had thrilled her so, now seemed like an evil, wicked grin. She grabbed his right arm and thrust it over her head so she could get away. Quickly she opened the car door and jumped out.

"Come back here," Tom yelled. "We can go away where your folks can't find us. Come on now, do you hear me? I love you, Polly."

His voice sounded demanding, something Polly never detected before. She ran on, not knowing where she was going, anywhere but back to him. When she saw Tom following, staggering along, she jumped behind a tree.

She was not alone. There was a rattling noise right at Polly's feet. Then it happened, too fast for her to get away. The snake struck her leg, sure and quick. Polly looked in horror as the viper slithered away.

"Tom," she yelled. "Tom, help me! Help me!"

Tom was not entirely sober, but he heard terror in Polly's voice and rushed toward her voice.

"What is it?" he asked as he reached her side.

"A snake bit me." Polly was quivering. One look told the story.

"A rattler!" Tom declared. "Come on, you need help fast."

20

Painfully Real

With Tom's support, Polly hobbled back to the car. Her leg was hurting dreadfully. Tom drove like he had never driven before.

"Where are you taking me?" Polly asked as they turned to the main highway. "Please take me home."

"You need a doctor right away. I can't take you home. There's no time to lose." Tom pushed the gas pedal even harder. In his less-than-sober state, he was weaving crazily down the road. Even in her panic, Polly heard a whine. A siren screeched somewhere in the distance. As the sound came closer, she noticed flashing lights.

Tom used language Polly didn't care to hear. She was shocked.

"Of all the rotten luck!" He pulled his car to the side of the road.

As the policeman approached his car,

Tom began to talk. "Officer, I can explain everything."

"Well, at the speed you were going, you'd better have a real good reason. Let me see your driver's license."

"We don't have time for that," Tom told him. "This girl has been snake-bit, and I'm on the way to the doc's."

As Tom talked, the officer could plainly detect the smell of liquor. He walked around to the other side of Tom's car and took a look at Polly.

"Looks bad," he observed. "Rattler, no doubt. Leave your car sit, and I'll take you on into town."

Tom had no idea what the policeman's plans were for him after Polly received help. Willingly they made the switch and were on their way. Never in her life had Polly driven as fast as they were driving now. Never had she heard such a loud noise as that siren. If only she had not sneaked out at night like this!

Back in the little house at this very hour, her mother felt a need to pray for her oldest daughter. Esther could not understand why, but she had a hunch that all was not well. Lately she'd noticed that Polly seemed different. At times she would be talking to Polly and she didn't seem to hear her. More than once Esther needed to ask, "Polly, did you hear what I said?"

It was as though her daughter was in a dream world of her own. Perhaps if Omar Troyers moved to Texas, Polly would be her own natural self again. She always enjoyed Omar's girls. Or better yet, maybe they would move back to Ohio, and then her children would be with friends and family again.

As the policeman pulled into town, he drove straight to the hospital.

"I thought we were stopping at Doc Warner's office," Tom objected.

"You ought to know the doctor wouldn't be in his office at this hour. Besides, the way that leg has swollen, she needs special attention," the officer declared.

Tom didn't argue.

At the hospital, Polly opened the door but could not walk.

"Wait here," the policeman told them. "I'll get help."

The doors soon opened, and a young man came to Polly's aid, pushing a wheelchair. They assisted her, and soon she found herself being pushed down a brightly lit hallway. Then the questions began.

"Name, please? Your age? What happened? Who brought you in? Parents' names? How can we reach them? Phone number?"

Then an elderly white-haired doctor appeared and began examining her leg.

"This needs attention right away," he assessed the situation. "Are her parents here?"

"No. We're trying to reach them," a nurse told him.

"Do all you can and quickly. We need to admit her."

It all seemed so unreal to Polly. If only it were a dream and she would wake up in her own bed in her own room. But it was painfully real.

Things began to fade out and look fuzzy. Someone was lifting her. Now she thought she was in a bed and the bed was floating far away. Polly felt peaceful and light. Then she knew nothing more as she drifted away into unconsciousness.

Esther had finally been able to fall asleep. The loud ringing of the phone brought her out of that first deep slumber. Mr. Olson had insisted that they leave the phone hooked up, but she had never gotten used to its jangle.

She wondered who would call at this hour. Then she felt a twinge of fright as she thought of her husband and son. Perhaps there had been an accident and one of them was hurt at the dairy barn. People can be injured so quickly on the farm. She certainly was not prepared for the message she received.

"I would like to speak to Mr. or Mrs. Ralph Miller, please," came the voice from the other end.

"I'm Mrs. Miller."

"Do you have a daughter by the name of Polly, seventeen years old?"

"Yes."

"I'm sorry to inform you, ma'am. This is Union Hospital at Laramie calling. Your daughter has been brought in with a snakebite. She has a serious reaction and must be treated immediately. The doctor needs your consent to admit her and give medical treatment."

"*Ach,* no," Esther exclaimed. "You're wrong. Polly has been in her room all night. She's sleeping."

"Please, ma'am, check and make sure," the nurse requested.

"*Waard mol* — I mean, wait once and I'll look." Esther laid down the receiver on the stand. She opened the door to her daughters' bedroom. Then she clutched at her throat, for Polly's bed was empty.

Rushing back to the phone, she confirmed the fact that Polly could be the girl about whom they called.

"Then we have your permission to do what we need to do for her?"

"Yes, you do," Esther declared.

"Thank you," the nurse said and hung up.

Esther's head felt as if it was spinning. She must get word to her husband. Later she was amazed that she remained calm enough to call Mrs. Olson and tell her to send Ralph home right away. Mrs. Olson detected alarm in Esther's voice and, after inquiring, found out the details.

"We'll bring Ralph over, and you get ready, Esther. I'll take you to the hospital myself."

Esther was grateful for her concern and help.

"How could this have happened?" Ralph asked his wife.

"I don't know. I thought she was in her room, asleep."

"Well, I'll get to the bottom of this. She'll have some explaining to do."

Esther didn't answer. Silently she prayed for her daughter's well-being.

21

Another Mystery

The ride to Laramie seemed endless. Esther kept wiping the tears that flowed so easily. Ralph sat rigid and silent, looking straight ahead. Once they reached the city limits, it was as if every traffic light turned red. Esther wished Mrs. Olson would drive faster, but the speed limit was much lower here in the city than it was on Highway Seven.

"We're just about there," Mrs. Olson announced, trying to comfort Esther. She couldn't understand why Ralph didn't try to console his wife. *Why, if it were me in Esther's predicament, my husband would take me in his arms and at least sympathize with me,* Mrs. Olson thought.

Neither she nor Esther knew of the struggle within Ralph's soul and mind. His heart felt as though it was pounding wildly. Ralph was concerned and hurting for his daughter, only he didn't know how to express it. He wished

135

Esther would stop crying. Ralph didn't like to see his wife cry. It made him feel so helpless.

"Your daughter will be okay," Roberta Olson tried to assure Esther. "I just know it."

"If it's God's will," Esther meekly replied.

"Well, why wouldn't it be his will? — a young girl like Polly, with all her life ahead of her. Surely God would want her to live. Anyway, nowadays the doctors have new medicines and ways to deal with these things. Don't worry."

None of them, not even Roberta Olson, were prepared for what they saw as they stepped into Polly's room. Surrounded by several nurses and a doctor, Polly lay pale and still.

The doctor looked up as they entered. "This your daughter?" He looked toward Ralph.

"*Ya,*" Ralph answered gravely, not trusting his voice.

"Please wait out in the lounge, and I'll be with you in a moment."

"But I must see her. I have to talk with her to find out what happened!" Esther begged.

The doctor nodded toward one of the nurses. She got the signal and took Esther's arm, leading her to the waiting lounge. "The doctor is doing all he can for your daughter.

We'll take good care of her and report her condition to you as soon as we can," the nurse told Esther.

"There's coffee in the cafeteria at the end of the hall. Why don't you have some? It will make you feel better."

But Esther didn't want coffee. She wanted her daughter. Why couldn't she see her now? What happened? How did she get here? So many questions needed an answer. Why must she wait?

Before long Esther saw Tom Dawson coming down the dimly lit hall. He looked frightened and disheveled.

"Tom!" exclaimed Ralph in surprise. "What are you doing here?"

"Don't you know?"

Ralph shook his head.

"Why, I brought Polly to the hospital, with the help of the police."

"Oh!" Esther exclaimed. "What happened? Why was she out at night? Where did you find her?"

"I didn't find her. She was out with me," Tom admitted. "We've been seeing each other for some time, and tonight I asked her if she would marry me.

"That seemed to frighten her, and she jumped from the car and ran. The next thing I knew, she was calling for help, saying a snake

137

bit her. That's when I found the police and brought her here."

Esther's legs would support her no longer. She sank down into a couch. Surely what Tom was saying wasn't true. But then Tom continued.

"Mr. Miller, I don't know about your ways, but Polly is a nice girl and deserves to get out more and have some fun. All she knows is work. I'd take good care of her. Will you let me have her for my wife?"

Ralph's face was almost livid. "Get out!" he muttered through clenched teeth.

"You have no right to live her life for her," Tom declared.

"Don't tell me what right I have concerning my daughter."

Tom took a step toward Ralph. He opened his mouth to further protest. At that instant Ralph detected alcohol on Tom's breath. "Leave us alone," he spat the words.

Mrs. Olson felt it was time to intervene. "Tom, you'd better go. Let's not cause any more problems. There has been enough trouble here tonight."

"Okay, okay." Tom backed off. "I'll go, but you wait and see!" With that remark Tom sauntered down the hallway and out of sight.

"I'm sorry," Mrs. Olson apologized. "I had no idea Tom was involved in this."

Five more minutes passed before the doctor made his appearance. "Your daughter will be alright," he stated. "Her snakebite was bad but not as deep as some I've seen. You have that young man to thank for bringing her in so promptly. Time is of great importance where snakebites are concerned.

"We have her on an IV and antibiotics, but she should be ready to go home in two or three days. You may go see her now, but no excitement. She needs to stay calm. I'll look in on her this afternoon again." With that, he shook Ralph's hand and left.

Esther was already by the hallway door, ready to go to Polly's room.

"I'll just wait here," Mrs. Olson offered. "You two go on ahead. I'm sure you want some time alone with your daughter. Maybe I'll have that coffee now."

Esther nodded to Roberta politely, wishing she would quit talking so they could go in to see Polly.

As they entered Polly's room this time, a nurse was adjusting something on her IV. Polly stirred. The nurse finished her duties and left the room.

"*Bist wacker* (are you awake)?" Mother asked.

Polly stirred again and opened her eyes. "*Dut weh* (it hurts)," she moaned.

139

Esther just stroked her daughter's forehead. It felt so hot. Few words were exchanged in the twenty-five minutes Ralph and his wife spent with Polly.

Finally the nurse appeared with the clothes Polly had been wearing when she was admitted.

"Here." She handed the package to Esther. "You may take your daughter's clothes home. She will be here a few days, and you can bring in a change of clothes for her to wear home."

Esther looked into the bag and exclaimed, "But these aren't her clothes!"

"Well, that's what we took off her when she arrived. You'll have to leave now so Polly can rest. Come back this afternoon if you like."

Bewildered, Esther walked out into the hallway. Here was another mystery she couldn't understand.

22

The Decision

The ride home was anything but pleasant for Esther. She wanted to go home only long enough to set things in order for her children to manage until Polly could be released.

"Can you bring me back this afternoon?" she asked Roberta Olson.

"Sure, I can do that."

"That's too much trouble," Ralph protested.

"Oh, no trouble at all, Mr. Miller."

"I want to stay with Polly until she can come home," Esther told her husband.

"Is that necessary? The nurses are taking care of her. That's what they get paid for." He was mentally calculating the cost of a hospital bill.

"But I must talk to Polly. There has to be some mistake. Look!" She pulled the green dress from the bag of clothes the nurse had given her and held it up for Ralph to see.

"This isn't Polly's dress. It's an *englisch* one, and there is no *Kapp* (head cap for Amish women and girls) in here. Polly never went anywhere without her *Kapp*. I just don't understand it."

"Why," exclaimed Roberta, "that dress belongs to my Rose Ann! However did it get to be in Polly's possession?"

"I aim to find out," Ralph promised.

"Can't I go back to the hospital this afternoon?" Esther asked. Her mother heart yearned for her daughter. There had to be a logical explanation. "She needs us now."

Ralph cleared his throat and looked straight ahead. He didn't say anything on the way home.

The other Miller children were anxiously waiting for their parents' return. Ben was the only one aware of the call during the night and the trip to Laramie. That was because he was working at the dairy when Ralph was given the message. He had told his siblings all he knew, which wasn't much.

As Mrs. Olson drove up to the Miller's house, she asked Ralph, "Well, shall I take your wife to the hospital this afternoon or not?"

Ralph glanced at Esther and saw a tear slowly trickle down her cheek. It touched him and he softly said, "*Ya,* you can."

"What time shall I be here?"

"Whenever it suits," Esther said with difficulty. "Here." She handed the green dress to Roberta.

Mrs. Olson reached out and took it. "Thanks. Okay, and remember, I'll pick you up at three o'clock, if that's alright."

"It will be good."

"Mom, how's Polly?" Ben, Sara, Levi, and Effie all seemed to talk at the same time.

"What happened? Where was she at that time of the night? How did she get to the hospital? Is she real sick? Will she die?"

Before Esther could stop the flow of questions, Ralph put an end to their inquiries. "*Genunk* (enough)! Polly will be in the hospital for a few days, but the doctor says she'll be alright. We don't know all the answers to your questions, but I intend to find out.

"Now I want it quiet around here. I didn't sleep all night, and I can't go to work this afternoon without some rest. Esther, try to keep things under control while I take a nap. Wake me around two-thirty."

"*Ya,* Ralph, I will." Esther ushered her family to the kitchen, explaining that she needed their help. "I'm going back to the hospital this afternoon. Maybe I'll stay until Polly can come home. So we need to plan meals for here and how you must help each other.

"Sara, you're twelve and old enough to go ahead with the cooking. Effie, you girls help each other with the washing. William, keep the wood box filled for the *Schtuppe-offe* (living room stove) and the ashes emptied.

"*Ach,* why am I standing here talking? Before I leave, we need to do some baking. I'll make cornbread and half-moon pies right away. Sara, get the fixings ready. Levi, build up the fire in the cookstove."

"But, Mom," Ben persisted, "what *did* happen to Polly?"

Esther knew her children were anxious about their sister, so she told them. "All I know is, she was out somewhere with Tom Dawson and got snakebit."

"Tom!" Ben gasped in surprise.

"We don't know how it all happened, but I couldn't sleep last night. Somehow it seemed I knew something was wrong. I prayed and prayed. I feel God heard those prayers and saved Polly from a danger worse than a snakebite."

"Was it a big snake?" Levi asked, "*en Rasselschlang* (a rattlesnake)?"

"Yes, Levi, it was a rattler, but I don't know how big. Now let's get busy. I have to get ready and do all I can before I leave."

William didn't want Mother to leave. Being the youngest, he whined and pouted. "Who'll take care of us, Mom?"

"Sara and Effie will take good care of you. Besides, now you are six and can do a lot to take care of yourself. Haven't you been helping around the house and even with some outside chores?"

"But I don't like for you and Dad to be gone. Why can't you take me along?"

"No, they wouldn't let you visit Polly in the hospital. You will be alright here, and it won't be long," Mother comforted him.

"We'll play checkers and *Schteckli* (hide and seek), and maybe I'll let you win," Levi offered.

Everyone was set to their tasks. Esther worked as fast and silently as she could. No one wanted to disturb Father's nap.

Mother gathered up Polly's hairpins, comb, and toothbrush to take along to the hospital. Looking in Polly's dresser drawers and closet, she found a change of clothing for her.

She mustn't forget anything, especially not her *Kapp*, she thought as she quickly put the articles in a paper bag.

Now she sat down with Sara and Effie and planned a menu for lunch and supper for three days. Breakfast was no problem. The family was content with a good helping of their usual mush, eggs, and tomato gravy.

However, in early afternoon the men

wanted a hearty meal of meat and potatoes before working second shift at the dairy.

Mother would send some sandwiches and half-moon pies along for their seven o'clock break. Esther often tired of such a strange schedule, but if it meant helping her husband pay off their farm sooner, she tried to cooperate patiently.

The children helped willingly. Soon it was time to wake Father, and then Esther would need to leave.

"Here's your supper, Ralph." Esther set the hot food on the table.

"The girls and I made out a menu for each meal while I'm gone. They will do alright. If I could have some money, I could call home once in a while and let you know how Polly is doing. And I suppose I need a little to buy something to eat," she noted wistfully, looking at Ralph.

"*Well, wie viel brauchst du* (well, how much do you need)?" Ralph asked.

"I don't know, not much I guess." Esther was not used to handling money.

Ralph carefully counted out a few dollars and handed them to her. "There's Mrs. Olson now, so go, if that's what you want. I know one thing: we are moving back to Ohio.

"After all I heard last night — yes sir, we're moving back."

23

Anything You Say

Esther's emotions were stirred. She was worried and sad because of her daughter's experience. Yet she was also glad because Ralph had declared they were moving back home to Ohio.

Had she just imagined it that he said that? Did he really mean it? She knew her husband never said anything unless he meant it. Did she dare tell Polly?

"You are so quiet," Mrs. Olson observed, breaking into Esther's thoughts. "Well, if you're still wondering why your daughter was wearing my Rose Ann's dress, my daughter cleared up that matter. Rose Ann has so many nice clothes to wear. She felt sorry for Polly and wanted to share with her."

"Polly has enough dresses." Esther tried not to sound ungrateful. She didn't want pity from anyone, especially if there was no need for it.

"No doubt she does, but not pretty ones. They're all drab, dark colors and made over the same pattern. Young girls like pretty things, and they need to have a bit of fun sometimes. I suspect that's why Polly was out with Tom. Too bad she had to sneak out!" Roberta Olson finished.

"Our way is different," Esther told her friend. "You don't understand."

"No, I certainly don't."

This was an opportunity for Esther to explain. "We are not put here on earth to have a good time or enjoy ourselves with worldly things. We don't dress fancy to draw attention to ourselves. The Bible says we should adorn ourselves with a meek and quiet spirit." Esther surprised herself by the confidence she had in speaking her mind.

"Well, I admire you for your belief, but I could never live like that."

Esther wondered if she couldn't or wouldn't, but decided it wasn't worth mentioning.

"Here we are," Roberta announced, easing the car into a parking space. "Give me time to lock my door, and I'll help carry your bags. My, are you planning to stay a month?" Mrs. Olson laughed.

"I want to stay until Polly comes home."

"That may be a while," Roberta told Esther. Realizing that was not an encouraging remark, her friend quickly tried to remedy her statement. "Of course, Polly is young. I bet she'll bounce back in a hurry!"

"I hope so," Esther responded.

Polly was wide awake when her mother and Mrs. Olson stepped into her room.

"Care for some visitors?" Roberta asked, smiling. "It looks as if we're moving in." Mrs. Olson laughed.

"Mom, I want to come home," Polly declared, totally ignoring Mrs. Olson's good-humored remarks. She didn't mean to be rude or unkind, but she was uneasy in the strange surroundings.

"We'll have to wait until the doctor says you may," Mother told her.

"Are you feeling any better, Polly?" Roberta asked.

"I think so, but my leg still hurts something *wunderbaar* (wonderful, fierce)."

Mrs. Olson had never heard of anything hurting "wonderful," but she suppressed any laughter. "Well, I hope you feel better real soon. Maybe I should go now, and I'll look in on your family every day, Mrs. Miller. Don't you worry about them. And when you're ready to come home, give me a call. I'll be right down. If the mister wants to come, we'll see he gets here."

"Thank you," Esther responded.

With this remark, Roberta Olson left for home.

A nurse came in and checked Polly's vital signs. "Mrs. Miller, are you staying for the night?" she inquired.

"Yes, I want to."

"That's fine, but you'll have to stay in the lounge. Since this is a semiprivate room, we cannot allow guests to spend the night with their patients."

"How late may I stay with my daughter?"

"Until eight o'clock. That's when our regular visiting hours are over."

"Alright. I'll sleep in the lounge then," Esther replied.

Finally, Polly and her mother were alone. "Polly, do you feel good enough so I can comb your hair and put it up? You need to wear your *Kapp*."

"Oh, Mom, *ich duh eenichebbes das du saage duhst* (I'll do anything you say). I wish I wouldn't have sneaked out."

Polly became restless. Beads of sweat appeared on her forehead.

"Maybe you'd better not talk now," Esther suggested. "You might upset yourself. We want you to get well as fast as possible."

"Mom, I have to. I must tell you how *arig* (bad) I've been. I wanted to wear *englisch* clothes, let my hair down, go without a *Kapp*, and all the things forbidden to us.

"Tom Dawson was so kind to me. He took me to the rodeo and other fun places. Ben and I are old enough for *Rumschpringe*, but we had no place to go. There aren't enough Amish families with grown *Yunge* (young folks) here yet.

"Tom told me that I'm pretty. No one ever told me that, except Rose Ann when I was dressed in her clothes. And then Tom asked me — oh, Mom, I don't know how to tell you —"

"Then just rest a while. You are getting all upset and nervous."

"No, Mom, let me tell it. I don't think I can sleep tonight if I don't tell."

"Rest a little, then you can talk some more," Mother advised Polly.

For ten minutes the girl lay quietly staring at the ceiling. Her face was wet with tears. Esther took a cool, damp washcloth and gently sponged her daughter's warm forehead and wiped away those tears.

"Now let me go on, Mom. Last night Tom said he had something to tell me and a special place to take me. We went to Silver Lake, and he asked me to marry him. He proposed that we go away, and you would never find us.

"Then he got a bottle of wine for us to drink

and celebrate, and he wanted to give me a ring. When I knew he'd been drinking, I tried to get away. He put his arm around me. I don't know how, but I got away and ran. He followed, and I tried to hide behind a tree.

"Just then I heard a funny rattling sound. I looked down, and by the bright moonlight, I saw this big, ugly snake. Quickly I tried to step back, but it happened so fast. The bite felt like a hot stove poker. I saw the snake crawl away.

"Oh, Mom, to think that I might have run away and married Tom if I wouldn't have seen him drunk and heard him talk so rough. I never want to see him again."

"God surely heard my prayers," Esther murmured.

"You mean you knew I was dressing up fancy and sneaking out with Tom?" Polly asked, amazed.

"No, but somehow I felt all was not as it should be, and I prayed a long time last night."

"Can I ever be baptized and be a good girl? Will you and Dad forgive me?"

"Yes, yes, I'm sure, Polly. Now rest, and once you're better, I'll tell you some good news. You've had enough excitement for one day."

However, there was more disturbance to come. Twenty minutes later Tom Dawson walked into the room.

Esther saw her daughter tense up. How she wished her husband were here. What should she do?

"Hello," Tom greeted them, smiling broadly.

Polly turned her face to the wall and said nothing. What an awkward situation this was!

24

Not Meant to Be

Tom removed his big hat, laid it on a chair, and with two long strides was at Polly's bedside.

"How are you feeling?" Tom asked.

Polly didn't answer.

Turning to Esther, Tom wondered, "Can't she talk? What's wrong with her?"

Mrs. Miller wished he would go away, but he didn't. Tom waited for an answer.

"I guess she just doesn't feel like talking. Maybe we had better let her rest," Esther replied.

"Well, I want you to know I'm sorry for everything that happened. I didn't mean any harm to your daughter. She's a beautiful girl, and I love her. I do hope you and your man will let me have her."

What kind of talk is this, thought Esther. *You don't say right out that you love someone. That's* kindish *(childish). You just love, but you don't have to say it.*

Getting no response from Mrs. Miller, Tom decided to come back later in the evening. "Maybe Polly will feel like talking later on," Tom told Esther. "I'll be back for evening visiting hours."

Esther breathed a sigh of relief as Tom left.

"I have nothing to say to him," Polly sobbed. "What shall we do if he comes back?"

"I will thank him for bringing you here and tell him you don't feel like talking yet."

"But, Mom, we can't keep this up *immer* (forever)."

True to his word, Tom did come back that evening. Esther met him at the door of Polly's room and told him what she said she would.

"I must talk to your daughter," he declared, brushing his way past Esther.

"Polly," Tom began, "I want to say how sorry I am. I wouldn't hurt you for the world. I love you too much to cause you any grief.

"Tomorrow I'm riding for big stakes in the rodeo. I've got a real good chance of winning. We can make big plans with the money. I'm gonna win, so you just hurry and get well. I'll be back tomorrow with the good news."

Tipping his hat, he gave them good-bye and sauntered down the hall, swaggering like a rodeo star.

Polly was fretful and restless. When the nurse checked her temperature, she had a fever. "What's wrong?" the nurse asked. "Did something upset her this evening?"

"Yes, someone did," Esther reported. "That Tom Dawson keeps coming to see her, and she doesn't want to talk with him at all."

"Oh, you mean the young man that brought her here? Well, we can fix that. I'll see that a NO VISITORS sign is posted."

"Thank you." Esther was grateful.

"I'm afraid he'll try to get in here anyway and cause problems," Polly groaned. "He can be determined."

"Let's not worry about that tonight," Esther comforted her daughter. "Do you think you could take some good news?"

"*Ya, ich kann* (yes, I can)."

"Well, alright then. Last night Dad announced that we're moving back to Ohio."

"Really, Mom? Does he mean it? Moving back home — back to our cousins and my friends Rachel and Lydia and Louella and Ada! Oh, Mom, really? When?"

"I don't know for sure, but I think *glei* (soon)."

"This is better than any medicine they could give me. Now I know I'll be out of here soon!" Polly exclaimed.

"Don't get too worked up. It's not good for you," Mother cautioned her.

"*Ich schlofe beilewe net* (I won't sleep at all),"
declared Polly.

Despite the worry about Tom coming back
the next day and the joyful news of moving
home, Polly did sleep.

Esther spent a good part of the night in
prayer for Polly and her family at home. She
also prayed that her husband could find it in
his heart to understand his children's need for
friends and to forgive Polly for sneaking out at
night with an *Englischer*.

"Well, young lady," commented Dr. Stahl
the next day after examining Polly. "I don't
know what happened here. If by tomorrow
you make as much of a change as you did
overnight, you'll be home before you know
it.

"Last night I was worried about that fever,
but a miracle has taken place. Someone must
have prayed." He shook his head and left the
room.

Esther knew Who had sent a miracle, an
answer to her prayers.

Late that evening there was a commotion
across the hall from Polly's room.

"They're moving someone in," Esther reported from the door. "It looks like a young
man. He sure is bandaged up . . . must have
been in an accident. That's one thing about
buggies: they don't go so fast, and if you

wreck, you just get bumped most of the time."

In a short while the nurse appeared and reported, "We have a young man across the hall who told us to tell you he'll be okay. He says he's your boyfriend. Do you know a Tom Dawson?"

Polly was startled. "Yes, I know him, but he's not my boyfriend."

"I didn't think so," the nurse remarked, "you being Amish and all. Oh, I'm sorry. I didn't mean to offend you. It just didn't seem likely."

"That's alright," Polly answered. "What happened? Is he hurt bad?"

"He was hurt riding in the rodeo. It happens all the time. We get these wild, young fellows in here who are tearing up their bodies for a few dollars and a flash of glory. He has a broken leg and some ribs fractured and a dislocated shoulder. That will keep him laid up for a while. Is there anything I should tell him for you?"

"Tell him we will pray for him," Esther stated.

"I hope you'll pray for enough good sense for him to stay away from bull riding after this," commented the nurse as she left.

Esther just murmured, " 'God moves in a mysterious way.' "

The next morning, Polly had continued to improve so much that the doctor let her go home with instructions: "Take it easy for a while, but gradually get a little more exercise each day."

She had tried walking the day before, with her mother's help.

"I believe I'll call home and tell them the good news," Esther told Polly. While she was on the phone, she told Sara to call Mrs. Olson and ask for her to come and pick them up at the hospital. She knew Roberta would be glad to do that since she had called once each day and assured Esther that everything was fine.

The day was dark and rainy, but for Polly it was bright with hope. She was going home. Although she dreaded facing her father, she need not have. Unknown to her, Ralph had made some changes, also.

She put on the Amish clothes her mother had brought to the hospital, and she donned her *Kapp*.

"Tom wants you at least to stop and say good-bye," the nurse told Polly. "He has been asking about you."

"Guess it can't hurt," Mother consented.

Slowly and shyly, Polly limped into Tom's room. How different and helpless he looked. "I came to say good-bye, and I hope you'll soon be well."

"Thank you," Tom responded. "I'm sorry for what happened to you and that it didn't work out for us. But I guess it wasn't meant to be. Good-bye, Polly, and good luck."

It really was easier than Polly expected. She turned and followed her mother and Mrs. Olson to the welcome sight of the outdoors.

25

Going Home!

Polly dreaded facing her father. "Oh, Mom, *was sagt der Dat* (what will Dad say)?" she asked.

After that first time, Ralph never once came to see his daughter at the hospital. His reason was that he was too busy on the dairy and making arrangements to move back home to Ohio.

Ralph told Esther to let the hospital know to send all bills to him, and he would take care of them.

"Polly," shared her mother, "Dad seems to have changed. I don't believe he'll scold you. We'll talk about it later." She didn't want to say too much in front of Mrs. Olson.

"So you are really leaving us?" Roberta Olson remarked.

"*Ya*, I guess so," Esther replied.

"We're sorry to lose such a hardworking family."

Esther didn't answer right away. She couldn't say she was sorry to leave. That would have been an untruth. But she did think to say, "We thank you for taking care of us so well when we arrived and for helping us through this crisis."

"Oh, that's okay. My husband is trying to find another Amish family to take your place. He's heard that a family from Indiana is interested in moving to Texas. I hope we get them. Your people are such good folks, hard workers, dependable."

"We have our faults," Esther replied.

"Being proud certainly isn't one of them. You don't seem to be able to accept a compliment."

Ralph and the children saw the car pull up the driveway. Her children stood in wide-eyed wonder as their mother and sister approached the house. Both of them looked so frail and tired.

Esther had eaten little, saving her money for phone calls to check on the rest of her family. During those conversations with her husband, she sensed a change in him. He took much of the blame for Polly's behavior. Esther never told her daughter. She wanted Ralph to talk to Polly himself.

"Dad, I'm sorry I went with Tom" were the first words Polly said as she stepped into the kitchen. "*Ich waar letz* (I was wrong)."

"*Ya,*" Ralph answered, "*du waar letz* (you were wrong). But I see now where I put paying the farm off first, ahead of my family. I should not have taken you away from all the *Freindschaft* (relatives) and the church. You needed friends. *Mir gehn zerick* (we're going back)."

Later Polly told her mom, "Oh, Mom, I thought he would scold me!"

Several weeks passed before Ralph received a reply from Amos Beachy. The answer pleased him. Amos wrote that he could vacate the place within six months if Ralph could wait that long.

"I thought we might be able to move sooner, but I suppose six months is a reasonable time to give Amos to make other arrangements. Just remember, Polly, you do not go out with an *Englischer*. Soon we'll be with our own people again, and you'll have enough company."

"*Ya,* Dad, I understand. Ben and I will be able to *rumschpringe* with the other *Yunge* (go out with the other young folks), but we don't want to be wild. I've had enough wild to know where it leads."

Those next six months were busy ones. Somehow it seemed as though time stood still. Yet at other times, there weren't enough hours in a day to get everything done.

"I do believe we have twice as much to take back," Esther remarked as she began packing.

The children eagerly helped. The task would be easier now that the little ones were of school age and could do more jobs.

"Just think," Ben remarked to Polly, "we'll be *rumschpringing*."

"Yes," his sister replied, "and we won't be going in secret behind Mom and Dad's back."

"I often wonder what it was about the church back home that Dad disapproved of, anyway," Ben commented.

"Mom told me he thought the *Yunge* (young folks) were getting too worldly. You know, some dressed too fancy, and a few wanted rubber tires on their buggies. Others had phone booths placed by the roadside near their homes. But I don't know why that matters anymore. We have been using modern conveniences here."

"That's true, Polly. Do you think we'll miss them?" Ben asked.

"Maybe at first, but I'll gladly do without them in exchange for being with our family again. Grandpas and our cousins will be so glad to see us."

"I hope so," Ben responded.

"Of course they will. I had a letter from

Louella Frey, and she wrote that everyone is anxious for us to come."

"Not any more anxious than we are to get there," Ben assured his sister.

Time for departure finally came. Sylvanus Yoders and Noah Yutzys came to help with last-minute packing and cleaning.

"We hate to see you go," Mrs. Yutzy told Esther.

"Yes, we sure do," Mrs. Yoder agreed. "We need you here to help build up the church."

"Your children are small yet," Esther replied. "Once they get older, they need friends and family ties. Don't stay away too long, unless some of your relatives and many more Amish move in. It doesn't pay."

The women wondered what Esther meant by that statement.

"Thank you for all your help," Ralph told them. "We will be leaving early in the morning. *Ich winsche alliebber euch gute* (I wish you all well)."

The Yoders and Yutzys conveyed their well-wishes and good-byes, then left. Now the Miller family began to organize the last steps for their departure.

"Mrs. Olson will take us to the train station at six. We need to get to bed so we can be up and pack last-minute things. Let's not keep Olson waiting."

Although everyone went to bed early, sleep eluded the children.

"What do you think it will be like?" Sara asked Polly.

"What are you talking about?"

"Why, to live in our old home again!"

"*Du glee Gans* (you little goose)," laughed Polly. "It will be *wunderbaar* (wonderful)."

"*Schtill datt drin* (quiet in there)," their father called out.

The girls knew they had better obey. Snuggling down under the covers, they closed their eyes tightly.

Too soon came the call, "Polly, Sara, come on. Get up."

Polly couldn't believe it was already morning. "*Was Zeit is es* (what time is it)?" she asked her mother as she rubbed her eyes.

"Four o'clock. We have to fix a bite to eat, pack some food for our trip, and clean up the kitchen. We don't want to leave a dirty kitchen, do we?"

They certainly wouldn't do that! Everyone hustled and bustled around, and by the time Mr. Olson came, they were ready.

"I'll take your furniture to the freight depot tomorrow and get it shipped out. Too bad you can't take your horse along, but I'm sure I'll find a good buyer for you. In fact, the Amish family coming from Indiana to replace you will probably need a driver."

"Thank you, Mr. Olson. I appreciate that."

"You and your family worked hard for me, and it's the least I can do."

Daylight was just stealing across the land as the train pulled into the station. Ralph ushered his family from the waiting room out to the platform. He was anxious to board and be on their way.

To everyone's surprise, there on crutches stood Tom Dawson. A young blond girl was clinging to his arm.

"We heard you all were leavin' this morning, so we just came to say good-bye." He flashed that big smile he loved to display.

"Well, we don't have time to talk to you and your sister. Train's leaving soon," stated Ralph.

"My sister!" Tom laughed. "This is my girlfriend, Stella Ames."

Polly's dad heard her gasp in surprise. He stepped between Tom and Polly and urged her briskly, "Get on the train, Polly."

Polly obeyed. She chose a seat far away from the platform to avoid any glimpse of Tom. *How can Tom pretend he cared for me and then come to show me his new girlfriend?*

Although Polly felt sore, she told herself that she didn't care anymore. She was glad when her family was all settled and the train began to move, toward Ohio, toward home, toward friends tried and true.

Her mother's prayers had indeed been answered. They were going home at last!

The Author

Raised in the fertile farming community of Plain City, Ohio, Mary Christner Borntrager was one of ten children. Her family was of the Amish faith. At the age of nineteen, she married John Borntrager.

Mary's education consisted of eight grades of elementary schooling. After leaving the Amish, she attended teacher-training institute at Eastern Mennonite College, Harrisonburg, Virginia. For seven years she taught in a Christian day school. After receiving a certificate in youth social work from the University of Wisconsin, she and her late husband worked with emotionally disturbed and neglected youth.

Borntrager is a member of the Ohioana Library Association and the author of seven novels in the Ellie's People Series: *Ellie*, *Rebecca*, *Rachel*, *Daniel*, *Reuben*, *Andy*, and *Polly*. She is in demand as a public speaker, was interviewed on local TV and radio, and receives many warm letters from her fans.

A member of the Hartville (Ohio) Mennonite Church, Borntrager lives at North Canton. Her hobbies include writing poetry, reading, quilting, memorizing the Bible, playing table games, and embroidering. She enjoys family get-togethers with her four children, their spouses, eleven grandchildren, and three great-grandchildren.

Mary hopes her series, Ellie's People, will bring pleasure to many readers and a better understanding of the Amish and their way of living.